THE LOOP

Where desire becomes data

D.R. MANAGO

First Edition
ISBN: 979-8-9955381-0-3
Cover design by D.R. Manago
Published by D.R. Manago

To my dear friend Nina,

who believed I could do anything,
if I wanted to.

For Anne—

your insight sharpened these pages, your questions made them braver, and your steady belief carried me through the long middle. You have been a mentor in craft, a coach in discipline, and a true friend when the story—and I—needed both.

For Teri—

thank you for your generous eye, your honest notes, and the warmth of your encouragement. Your friendship is felt in every strengthened line.

For Rick—

friend, thoughtful reader, and steady supporter. Your willingness to step into the early versions of this story helped shape what it eventually became.

For my family—

you are the ground beneath every risk I take. Your love gives me the courage to imagine worlds and the strength to return home.

And for my partner—

you are my calm, my spark, and my constant. This story exists because you believed in it—and in me—before it ever had a shape.

THE LOOP

Where desire becomes data

PROLOGUE

Derek stood in the kitchen, listening to the house settle. The tumbler Brandon used still sat on the counter, untouched. Derek hadn't moved it. He told himself it was practical—that he would pick it up when Brandon came back. The silence didn't feel final.

"Artemis," he said quietly. "Play back Brandon's last message."

I just need a little space. I'm not disappearing.

Derek let it finish. Then played it again.

The words didn't change. The tone didn't change. That same softness at the end, careful, intentional—meant to reassure.

It didn't.

Three months had passed since they last saw each other. Their final night had been controlled. Measured. Everything said indirectly. Everything held back.

At the door, Brandon had kissed him softly, unhurried and not hesitant. Familiar in a way that made it worse. He lingered just long enough to leave something behind.

Something that didn't leave.

The penthouse still held his scent: citrus, clean linen, the quiet weight of presence that hadn't faded. His hoodie was draped over the chair in the bedroom. Derek hadn't touched it.

He stepped toward it, then stopped.

Don't push.

He knew that rule. Pressure didn't bring Brandon closer. It made him disappear.

Space wasn't leaving. That's what Brandon had said.

Derek wanted to believe it.

The toothbrush was still there. The shampoo. Small, ordinary proof of continuity.

And still, something in his chest tightened, like he had missed a step and only now felt the drop.

He checked the time.

Too early to message. Too late to pretend he didn't want to.

He sat at the counter, hands folded, jaw set. He wasn't helpless. Just… holding. Waiting.

Whatever Brandon was doing, wherever he was, Derek stayed exactly where he was, balanced between patience and need, between trust and the quiet fear that nothing would change.

CHAPTER ONE

The Party

He sensed it before he saw it, the house seeming to take a breath as he arrived.

The gate scanned his license. Soft light glowed beneath the car as the system read the ID, and an uneasy awareness settled in his chest, as if the house had already judged him.

Artemis parked among electric cars that looked more like sculptures than vehicles. Brandon stayed in his seat for a moment, gripping his camera bag. Breathe. Observe. Keep your distance. Don't get involved. Nerves pricked anyway.

Ahead, the Klein mansion shimmered, glass panels changing in tone and brightness, responding to something deeper than light. Tonight wasn't about the party. It was about proving he could stand in the same room as Derek without unraveling. Brandon had rules. Not moral. Not philosophical.

Functional.

Don't let the Loop open in public.

Don't drink anything you didn't watch get poured.

Because when his judgment slipped, the Loop didn't seek permission.

A memory surfaced: a bar, a stranger, a drink he hadn't watched being made, the Loop opening too quickly, a guy clutching his chest.

Brandon exhaled slowly, grounding himself.

Don't mistake familiarity for safety.

For a moment, the Loop shifted—not opening, just… testing the edges.

The Loop sat under his sternum, low and constant. It amplified everything—joy, fear, desire—and once it opened, it didn't stop.

It intensified, so he kept it closed—always.

Derek had been the exception. Not because it was safe. Because it wasn't.

What he shared with Derek wasn't romance. It was data.

The camera strap across Brandon's chest settled into place. Familiar. Reliable.

He stepped out of the car into air thick with citrus, ocean, and wealth. A Synthetic Human greeted him at the entrance, its name glowing faintly.

"Welcome, Mr. Adams. Would you like a cocktail? Elexa. Citrus ginger. Gentle onset."

"Sure."

A drink gave him something to hold. Something physical.

The Synth hesitated. Its pupils contracted, recalibrating. A fraction too long. Long enough to notice.

Something in his chest tightened, subtle and instinctive, then it eased.

"Enjoy your evening."

Brandon took the glass without looking back. Still, hesitation lingered with him.

Inside, the house was alive. The walls displayed shifting art, tidal patterns, molten shapes, and heat maps that responded to music. The space belonged to Thomas Klein, which meant the party was never just a party.

When Klein hosted, something was being tested.

Glass shifted from clear to tinted. Conversations sounded meaningful but rehearsed. Laughter landed perfectly. Everyone watched. While pretending not to.

Synths moved through the crowd with dancer-like precision, catching spills before they happened, refilling glasses before they emptied. Everything gleamed. And beneath it all, a faint chill.

Brandon hadn't wanted to come. Seeing Derek made it worse. As he moved through the room, anxiety grew, not suddenly, but gradually increasing with each step.

Standing here, knowing he couldn't avoid it, was the part he wasn't prepared for. Seeing him again. Not knowing what it would bring.

What frightened him most wasn't the encounter itself. It was the possibility that Derek might still feel like home.

He raised his camera.

The viewfinder narrowed the world.

People revealed their true selves when they thought no one was watching. He noticed a woman with a shaved head leaning into her sequined partner, and a couple flirting as they pretended to argue about philosophy.

Click.

Truth, unguarded for a second, before it closed again.

Click.

And then, he felt it. Something pulled low in his chest. A tremor of memory.

"Hey there, handsome."

Derek Klein entered his space with the ease of someone who had once belonged there. The grin hadn't changed. Dangerous. Effortless. Meant for him.

Brandon hated that his body reacted before his mind did. Warmth spread through his chest, not from the drink but from Derek. Before he could think, his posture mirrored his feelings. Old patterns resurfaced. His breath quickened.

No. Control yourself.

He shifted his weight, grounding through his heels. Sensation is information, not a command. He forced the thought to stick. Still, the warmth lingered, desire threaded with irritation, with defense, with something not yet settled.

They moved through the party together. Conversation flowed easily. Too easily. Familiar to the point that the lines blurred. It's part memory, Brandon thought, as he glanced toward the wall display, and part lingering desire.

Metallic light washed across Derek's chest, turning it gold. Brandon raised his camera. Three quick shots. The third one captured Derek unguarded. Looking directly at him.

Clear.

Unprotected.

That one he'd keep.

Music swelled from the great room as a Synth bartender spun bottles through the air, smooth as planets in orbit.

"Put your camera down for a while, handsome," Derek said. "Dance with me."

Brandon hesitated.

Then—"Here we go…" Brandon muttered under his breath.

They drank. They danced. They laughed. Derek pointed out who was who with easy confidence, and for a while, Brandon let the night blur around them.

Then Derek leaned in. "Let's get some air."

The balcony opened toward the dark Pacific, unaffected by the party's theatrics. Brandon rested his hand on the railing, feeling its chill grounding him. They stood close. Very close. Derek radiated warmth like a memory.

"You miss it?" Derek asked.

Brandon kept his eyes on the water. "Miss what?"

"How we were."

Brandon's body tensed as his mind caught up. Longing conflicted with restraint.

"That," he said softly, "was the problem."

"Derek, we had an agreement."

"Let's not stay in the past," Derek said. "Let's just… decide what comes next."

The Loop stirred. Listening. Brandon pressed two fingers lightly to his sternum. Stay quiet. Don't let it take over now, he thought.

Derek moved closer. His breath brushed Brandon's cheek. Then, with a subtle, purposeful pressure, he pressed the bulge of his arousal against Brandon's thigh.

"Tell me you don't think about us."

Brandon didn't answer.

A soft scream echoed from the garden, a Synth intercepting a spill. Brandon felt a tingling sensation behind his sternum.

Derek's hand moved to his waist. Brandon remained still. He should have stepped back, but he didn't. Then Derek kissed him.

The kiss felt like a question. Memory wrapped warm and slow around them, familiar enough to be dangerous.

Brandon responded before he could stop himself. His pulse raced, and desire hit him hard. His hand moved across Derek's back, pulling him closer, and the Loop surged open. Emotion doubled. Pleasure hit back even harder, amplified and instant.

He struggled to close it, emotions overwhelming him as his body trembled. Gradually, the wave of emotion subsided. He pulled away, sacrificing raw vulnerability for steady breathing.

If he left it completely open, Derek wouldn't just experience pleasure. He'd feel everything.

The intensity softened. The kiss became imperfect. Human again. Brandon's breath came unsteadily as he tried to gather himself.

Derek held his gaze. "Still happens like that?"

"The Elexa," Brandon said casually. "It's pretty strong."

Derek's mouth curved, but his eyes didn't. "You always did understate it."

Desire tangled with restraint, lingering long after Derek stepped away. Brandon allowed himself to feel it, then took a steadying breath. He stayed on the balcony, letting the ocean breeze cool him.

Inside, the party went on without them. Simon showed up. "The citrus course is being served."

Derek nodded. "Coming." He glanced back once before disappearing into the room.

Brandon remained in place, allowing the ocean to draw him back into himself.

CHAPTER TWO

Indiscretion

By the time the music wound down and most of the guests had left, Brandon realized he had spent the entire night orbiting Derek.

When Derek said, "You should stay," Brandon already had reasons to leave—history, logic, self-preservation—but the night had stirred something in him, something harder to ignore than any of those.

"Come with me," Derek said.

Brandon hesitated just long enough to know he should say no. Then he looked at him, felt his restraint loosen under the weight of alcohol and desire, and followed him upstairs.

The suite lighting shifted as they reached the door—warm, golden, intimate in a way that made every shadow feel purposeful, wrapping around them like a hand at the small of his back and guiding him forward.

The door clicked shut behind them.

He should have stopped there.

Instead, Derek reached for him first.

The moment their mouths met, something fractured open.

Desire hit hard, hot, familiar, immediate. Derek felt like a memory and like every decision Brandon had already decided he wouldn't make again, and his body responded without permission, falling into a rhythm it hadn't forgotten.

He drove them back toward the bed, hands already pulling at Derek's shirt.

Stopping would have required something he didn't have.

He didn't try. Not tonight. Not with Derek looking at him like that.

Clothes came off fast, no choreography, no thought. Fabric slipped away, zippers whispering as pieces of themselves fell to the floor like something already decided.

Derek moved slower. Deliberate. He didn't look away.

The space between them tightened.

Brandon felt it deep in his body, sharp, immediate, unavoidable. His pulse raced into his throat, his mouth dry as the thought surfaced.

This is going to cost me.

He didn't stop.

His hands found him anyway.

Derek climbed onto the bed with quiet confidence, knees parting, back arching just enough, an invitation that didn't need explaining. Then he moved closer, slow and certain, his mouth finding Brandon's again.

The kiss deepened, less hunger now, more surrender.

No words. Derek didn't need them.

A single gesture toward the nightstand.

Enough.

Brandon's body tightened in response, already there, already past deciding.

When Derek's hand closed around him, the contact pulled a broken breath from his chest.

Then his mouth followed.

Hot. Precise. Familiar enough to undo everything Brandon had tried to rebuild.

His knees nearly gave.

He kicked the last of his clothes away, reaching blindly, his hand unsteady now as every movement pulled him deeper, pleasure threaded with something darker, something quieter.

You don't get to have this. The thought surfaced. His body ignored it. He pressed forward, slow, heat, resistance, then deeper, until there was no space left between them.

Derek's breath broke.

The sound hit harder than the contact.

Brandon's body responded sharply and instantly, overwhelming in its intensity, and it didn't stay confined. It surged back through him, amplified, doubled, and pushed toward excess. He felt all of it. Every shift. Every response that wasn't entirely his.

He forced it down, closing the Loop hard enough it almost hurt.

The silence that followed inside him felt worse.

His body moved anyway.

Memory guiding.

The rhythm built, controlled, measured, holding the edge as long as he could. Derek met him there, precise, pushing back, tightening around him in ways that stripped thought down to instinct.

The sounds he made changed.

Softer.

Real.

That was what caught Brandon, the shift, the point where control would break.

He felt it coming.

The pull.

The edge.

He tried to hold it there, tried to slow it, contain it, keep it physical.

It wasn't.

Derek broke first—tension, then release, sharp and involuntary.

Brandon felt it. Not just contact. The echo. That was enough. It pulled him under with it.

His own release followed, hard, immediate, leaving no space to stop it. His grip tightened at Derek's hips as his body gave in.

Afterward, they collapsed together, breathing uneven, bodies still reacting. The room felt quieter now.

Derek's body curved naturally against his, familiar, and that was what Brandon hated most.

Not the sex. Not the loss of control. The way it still fit. The way it still felt right.

***

Sleep came before either of them could separate. Morning arrived without ceremony. The weight of it stayed.

Brandon woke first. The room felt different in daylight, less forgiving, less capable of holding what had happened. Derek lay beside him, loose and unguarded. Comfortable. As if nothing had changed.

Brandon stood and moved to the window, pressing his palm lightly against the glass. "I need to go," he said.

Derek didn't answer, only a soft, amused exhale from the bed. Then a casual, unbothered movement, and a moment later, his voice drifted from the shower, singing off-key Whitney Houston.

The contrast weighed heavily on Brandon's chest.

A shimmer flickered across the bedroom door.

A Synth stood behind it.

"Mr. Adams," Simon said gently. "Will you be joining us for breakfast?"

"No," Brandon said.

Brandon stood alone in the room.

The house adjusted around him, with lighting shifting and interfaces activating as systems recognized his presence. The nightstand illuminated when he touched it, a translucent interface emerging from the glass.

"Create a message," he said quietly.

The display opened. Recipient options hovered in minimalist script.

He hesitated.

Then: Derek Klein.

The cursor blinked.

He stared at it longer than he had looked at Derek's body the night before. Keep it simple. Clean. No ambiguity.

Derek,

Last night felt familiar. That doesn't mean it moves us forward.

I don't regret you. I just know who we are—and who we aren't.

Take care of yourself.

— B

He paused. Not perfect. But true.

"Send."

"Delivered," the system confirmed.

He powered the surface dark.

Dressed.

As he moved toward the door, the house lighting dimmed slightly, almost as if it were reacting to his departure.

He stepped into the hallway.

Stopped. Took a breath.

Then continued down the stairs.

Thomas Klein stood near the bottom.

Shirtless.

Silk lounge pants, revealing more than Brandon wanted to see this morning, composed in a way that made the setting feel intentional rather than casual.

"Heading out?" Thomas asked.

His tone was light.

Too light.

"Yeah," Brandon said. "Early start."

"Of course," Thomas replied, stepping closer—not enough to crowd, just enough to test.

"Great meeting you last night," he added. "I'll have my assistant arrange dinner. You, Derek, and me."

His hand brushed Brandon's shoulder.

Lingering.

Evaluating.

Brandon held still.

"Yes, sir," he said.

"Just Thomas," he corrected smoothly.

His gaze drifted—not subtle, not overt—just enough to register.

Then he stepped back. As if the moment had already given him what he wanted.

Outside, the morning air hit differently.

Cool.

Real.

Brandon asked Artemis to stop the car just beyond the gate. He leaned back, closing his eyes briefly as the gate slid shut behind him. The Loop hummed faintly beneath his ribs. He wasn't feeling pleasure or longing; it was something unresolved.

"I'm tired of carrying this," he murmured. He forced it down, layer by layer, until the hum quieted.

"Home," he said.

"Confirmed," Artemis replied. "Eight minutes."

As the mansion shrank behind him, the Seal Beach Pier glimmered. He almost rerouted, walking the pier, his ritual for scraping other people's fingerprints off his thoughts, but exhaustion was heavier.

By the time he reached his home, sunlight painted long shadows across the floor.

"You are home, Brandon," Artemis said.

He dropped his camera bag, kicked off his shoes. The Loop hummed, Derek's echo still beneath his ribs, fading into something dull and dangerous.

"Later," he muttered.

He stripped, crawled into bed, and let sleep take him as the scent of citrus, sex, and someone he couldn't keep blurred into quiet.

He wanted distance.

His body wanted the opposite.

CHAPTER THREE
Saturday Morning Reset

Brandon woke to light, not the gentle, programmed sunrise he normally queued—amber blending into peach—but something sharper. Midmorning. Unplanned.

His head throbbed, not from alcohol, but from feeling too much in too little time. He inhaled slowly, exhaled even slower. At least he was in his own bed. That mattered more than it should have.

Derek's laugh hovered on the edge of memory.

"Damn." The warmth of his mouth. The way his body had responded before his mind caught up. Brandon sat up carefully, feet finding the cool concrete floor. He braced his palms against the mattress until the room steadied.

"Nope," he murmured to the ceiling. Not denial. Protocol. "I am not doing this today."

He already knew mornings were when mistakes seemed heavier, when they stopped feeling temporary. The rule hadn't come from paranoia; it had come from experience.

***

The bar was loud, with bass pounding through his bones, heat thick with sweat, pheromones, and spilled alcohol. Brandon had been there with friends. Then he wasn't. That part didn't matter. He liked the edges anyway.

A guy had taken the empty stool beside him. Late twenties. Easy confidence. The kind of warmth people naturally gravitate toward.

"You look like you're observing the wildlife," the guy said.

Brandon smiled faintly. "Occupational hazard."

Two glasses appeared. "I already ordered for you," the guy added. "You looked like you needed something better than beer."

Brandon hesitated just long enough to notice it. Then, the glass was already in his hand, cold with bright citrus and a clean burn.

The guy's hand grazed his wrist. That was all it took.

The Loop opened.

At first, it felt like warmth—familiar and manageable. Then it doubled. Brandon sensed the guy's attraction—clear and straightforward. Soon after, the guy realized Brandon was noticing him. The response changed instantly.

Attraction sharpened, then grew stronger—then something else.

The guy leaned in closer. "You feel that?" he asked, smiling.

Brandon did. Too much. Heat surged through him rapidly, more than he could hold back. It wasn't just attraction anymore—anticipation, excitement, then confusion. And when confusion set in, everything escalated.

The guy stiffened, his hand going to his chest. "What the—"

Brandon tried to close the Loop. Too late. Fear entered the cycle. Reflected. Amplified.

The guy staggered back. "What did you do?"

Heads turned. The bartender leaned forward. "You okay?"

Brandon felt all of it—fear, embarrassment, and the sudden urge to escape. He sealed the Loop shut hard.

The echo collapsed. But the damage didn't.

The guy stood there, breathing unevenly, and looked at him like something had gone wrong.

"I'm fine," he muttered.

But he didn't look at Brandon again and left without finishing his drink.

Brandon stayed longer than he should have. The untouched glass sat in front of him, condensation slowly sliding down the side. It was one drink he hadn't watched being poured. One moment he hadn't controlled.

That was enough.

Back in the present, Brandon stood in his kitchen, the memory settling into place.

"Artemis," he said, voice rough. "Status."

"Saturday. 10:14 a.m. Outside temperature: sixty-eight degrees. Ocean visibility: high. You have one unread message from Derek Klein and three from Tiago Santiago."

"Mute Derek."

"Muted."

"Show me Tiago later."

He moved into the bathroom. The mirror brightened automatically, metrics appearing along the edge: hydration, stress, and neural activity. He ignored them, looking at himself instead.

"You look like shit," he said quietly. Swollen eyes. Faint redness at his mouth.

Evidence.

"It was a photo op," he added.

The lie sat there. Unchallenged.

He pressed two fingers to his sternum. The Loop answered, low, irritated, overextended.

"Yeah," he murmured. "I know."

The shower heated instantly. Water hit his shoulders with more force than needed. He scrubbed harder than necessary, as if friction could erase memories. Citrus scent filled the space. Steam blurred the glass.

Derek's voice slipped in anyway. Off-key Whitney Houston. Uninvited.

"Fuck."

Brandon shut his eyes. "No."

The Loop flickered. He forced it down.

Wrapped in a towel, he moved into the kitchen. "Biobrew," he said. "Espresso. Medium."

The machine hummed.

He picked up his camera. The weight immediately grounded him, steady, dependable, safe. Cameras didn't care what you felt. Only where you pointed them.

He didn't upload last night's photos. Not yet. Instead, he looked out the window. A thin strip of ocean between rooftops. The pier. Always the pier.

It wasn't about escape. It was recalibration.

He dressed simply—jeans, worn T-shirt, sandals. Nothing that drew attention. Nothing that invited interpretation.

At the door, he hesitated. Stay in. Answer Tiago. Think.

He considered it. Then dismissed it.

"I'm going," he said.

"Enjoy the walk," Artemis replied.

The air hit him clean—salt, traffic, distant voices. Three gulls perched on a power line across the street, perfectly spaced. Too perfect.

He frowned. One shifted. Another hopped. The pattern broke.

Brandon exhaled—and started walking.

CHAPTER FOUR

Interlude: Unseen Threshold

Brandon almost didn't notice it. That was the point. The expo stretched across three city blocks, with glass pavilions, floating projections, and controlled lighting designed to feel optimistic. Everything about it reassured: clean, intentional, safe.

Artemis had suggested he attend, citing high networking potential. He hadn't come for that; he had come for the light.

The atrium ceiling fractured the afternoon sun into shifting geometric patterns that moved across the concrete floor—subtle, constant, precise.

He raised his camera, tracked the movement, adjusted, and shot.

A robotics company unveiled an adaptive chassis nearby, its movement smooth enough to seem almost organic. A biotech startup showcased a skin interface gently pulsing beneath a model's collarbone.

Brandon saw it. Framed it. Captured it. Moved on.

Then he reached the Holotec display. And something shifted. Not in the room—inside him. A faint pressure settled beneath his sternum. His breath caught, just slightly.

The Loop stirred. Aware.

Brandon lowered the camera slightly. For a moment, the room seemed to flatten, voices dimmed, movement slowed, and the distance drifted out of sync. Then it went back to normal. He exhaled slowly.

"Probably nothing."

Above him, hidden within the structure, a sensor array adjusted. Background scans ran continuously, marketed as experience optimization, quietly sampling biological signals across the crowd. Most readings dissolved into noise. Brandon didn't.

His signal held, steady, coherent, unusual.

The system flagged it. Level Three anomaly. Unconfirmed.

Nothing looked different on the floor. No alarms. No interruptions. No one approached him.

Brandon moved toward a hydration station, pressing two fingers gently to his sternum. The sensation came back, softer but intentional. A low hum. Like something had sensed him.

He scanned the room without turning his head, letting his eyes move naturally. Conversations overlapped. Demonstrations continued. Light shifted across the floor.

Everything looked normal. Nothing felt off.

Nearby, a display cycled through branding visuals. A stylized gull appeared wings held in perfect symmetry. It held a fraction too long, then reset.

Brandon blinked and looked away. "Breathe and observe," he murmured. The feeling didn't go away. It receded. He lifted his camera again, got back to work, and let routine take over.

By evening, the expo felt distant, filed, processed, already fading. He uploaded the photos, made minor edits, and closed the set. Moved on. Or tried to.

***

Five miles away, Dr. Samantha Fox opened a flagged file. She read it once. Then again, more slowly.

BRANDON ADAMS

Tier III — Dormant

Confirmation Required

Status: Unconfirmed / Observe

Sam leaned back in her chair. Dormant Tier III signatures were rare and rarely held together this neatly. Her fingers rested lightly on the edge of the desk as she studied the file.

Outreach was possible, and so were the consequences. Attention always arrived faster than protection. She made the decision quietly: observe, no recruitment, no escalation, no contact. Let him live.

She marked the file. It closed with a soft, final click. Stored. Archived.

But not dismissed. Somewhere in the system, a quiet flag remained attached to Brandon Adams's signal—Dormant. Waiting.

CHAPTER FIVE

Pier Encounters

The pier smelled of salt and old wood, the kind that clung to your clothes long after you left.

The boards under Brandon's feet were faded gray, slick from years of footsteps, sun, and storms. He liked spots like this, where memories were imprinted on surfaces and remained there.

He paused at the railing, resting his forearms on the weathered wood as the sensor lights flickered on. The sun sat low, casting long streaks of gold and shadow across the planks.

Photographers chased this light. Brandon didn't chase it. He waited for it. Then he lifted the camera. A gull swept low, wings flashing white. He tracked it instinctively, finger hovering over the shutter, waiting for motion and balance to align.

"Careful," a voice said behind him. "They'll steal anything they think you're eating."

Brandon turned. The warning didn't startle him; it was the proximity that did. The guy stood close enough to be felt, balanced, not imposing.

"I wasn't," Brandon said automatically. "Eating, I mean."

The guy's mouth curved slightly, not quite a smile. "I figured. You're watching the light, not the birds."

That hit harder than expected. Brandon lowered the camera slightly. "You noticed."

"I tend to notice what people are paying attention to."

Brandon observed him.

Stillness. Weight evenly distributed. No unnecessary movement. Nothing reaching.

"Marcus," the guy said, offering his hand.

"Brandon."

Their hands met. Warm. Not a spark. Not a jolt. Just warmth.

Marcus released him almost immediately.

Brandon noticed that too.

Marcus turned back toward the horizon. "So, are you here to take pictures… or to avoid something?"

Brandon let out a quiet breath. "Is it that obvious?"

"It usually is."

Marcus leaned against the railing, leaving space between them. Not pulling away. Not closing in. Just allowing it.

"I come here to reset," Brandon said. "The light changes fast. It forces you to stay present."

Marcus nodded, eyes following the seam where ocean met sky. "You see in frames."

Brandon swallowed. "Yeah."

Marcus didn't look at him when he spoke again. "Does it ever get tiring? Breaking the world into pieces?"

The waves rolled beneath them, slow and steady.

"Sometimes," Brandon said. "But it helps me notice what matters."

He hesitated.

"Small things. The way hands move when someone's nervous. The way people's eyes tell the truth before they're ready to."

Marcus turned then. Not abruptly. Intentionally.

"And what do my hands say?"

Brandon glanced down before he could stop himself. Still. Open. Not reaching. "They say you're holding back."

A moment passed. Marcus didn't deny it.

"That's… accurate."

A gull landed on the railing a few feet away. Then another followed. Their bodies angled the same way. Watching.

Brandon frowned. "They've been doing that lately."

Marcus didn't answer right away. He watched them a fraction too long. "Yeah," he said quietly. "They have."

Something in his tone tightened Brandon's chest. They stood there for a while, conversation moving easily between silence and sound.

"What have you been working on?" Marcus asked.

Photography, mostly commercial. Light is tricky; change it, and everything shifts.

Marcus nodded, focused and present.

"What about you?"

"Legal counsel," Marcus said. "Executive level."

He shifted slightly. Not hiding. Just making a choice.

"Holotec," he added. "Thomas Klein."

The name hit, tightening something in his chest. Brandon felt it register but didn't react. He thought about Derek, about how easily this could change. He didn't say anything. Some information shifts the moment it's spoken. Better to let this one stay.

The wind shifted, pulling at Brandon's jacket. He shivered. Marcus moved, not toward him, just enough to block the wind—no contact. The warmth came anyway. Brandon's breath caught.

"You okay?" Marcus asked.

"Yeah," Brandon said.

Then, after a moment, "Just… surprised."

Marcus studied him carefully and intentionally. He lifted his wrist console. "I'll be here tomorrow around noon. There's a place down the pier that makes tolerable chowder."

Brandon looked at him. Is that an invitation?

"It's an option," Marcus said. "You don't owe me anything."

Something changed. Subtle but genuine. "I'd like that," Brandon said.

Marcus nodded once. Decision made.

As they parted, Brandon lifted the camera, not to take a photo but to steady his hands.

The Loop settled. Not closed, not open. Aware.

Brandon didn't walk far. The pier narrowed as the crowd moved on. The ocean remained. The encounter followed him, not just as a memory, but as a presence.

At home, he slipped inside and gently shut the door. His hand lingered on it a moment longer than needed. Marcus stayed lost in his thoughts in small, deliberate ways. "You're watching the light, not the birds." It wasn't a line. It wasn't a move.

It was true.

Brandon set the camera down, still unopened. The late light through the windows felt cooler now. Less forgiving. He leaned back. Exhaled.

Marcus hadn't reached. Hadn't pushed. Hadn't tried to move anything forward. And somehow, that made it harder to ignore.

Tomorrow. Noon. Chowder. The thought settled easily, no pressure, no expectation.

The Loop stirred quietly, present.

Brandon looked toward the window. Toward the pier just beyond his walls. Tomorrow wasn't a promise. But it was enough.

CHAPTER SIX

Midday Light

The next morning didn't quiet it. Brandon listened to his messages while the Biobrew worked.

Morning light moved across the house in uneven bands, slipping through the smart glass as it adjusted to the sun. He leaned against the counter, letting the warmth settle without fully relaxing into it.

Tiago first.

Hey. Just confirming tonight, drinks at seven, dinner after. The Point. Don't disappear on me.

Brandon smiled, something in his chest loosening.

Tiago's voice always did that, grounding him without asking anything in return.

Then Derek.

His thumb hovered over the message.

He felt it before he opened it.

A tightening. A shift.

He tapped it anyway.

"Morning," Derek said, voice warm, unguarded. "Just checking in about tonight. Same plan. Drinks at The Point, then dinner."

A breath. A soft laugh.

"I enjoyed us the other night. Let's do that again soon. It was nice… having time. Just you and me."

The message ended.

Brandon didn't move.

The room stayed quiet. The Biobrew clicked off behind him.

He set the device down slowly.

Didn't reply. Didn't delete it.

Some things carried weight whether you answered them or not.

***

By noon, the pier felt different, busier, louder, less forgiving. The light no longer softened anything; it revealed everything.

Brandon spotted Marcus before Marcus saw him. Leaning against the railing, with one foot crossed over the other, sunglasses pushed back into his hair. Relaxed but not careless. Present.

Marcus shifted as if he sensed the attention. Their eyes locked. Something calmed.

"You came," Marcus said.

"You promised tolerable chowder," Brandon replied. "I'm holding you to that."

Marcus smiled. Not rehearsed. Genuine. They ordered at the window and sat overlooking the water. The gulls moved constantly now, less precise, more opportunistic. The rhythm of the place had shifted with the crowd.

Brandon noticed it immediately.

Marcus noticed Brandon noticing it.

"So," Marcus said, setting his spoon down, "yesterday you were observing. Today… you're in it."

Brandon blinked. "Just me?"

Marcus nodded toward the camera strap resting against his chest. "You're not hiding behind it today."

Brandon considered that. "Feels a little exposed."

"I wondered," Marcus said.

They ate silently for a moment.

"You always watch people this closely?" Brandon asked.

Marcus glanced up. "Do you?"

Brandon smiled. "Fair."

A gull dropped onto the railing a few feet away. It cocked its head, watching Brandon's bread with calculated interest.

"Don't," Brandon said.

The gull didn't move.

"I think it's sizing you up," Marcus said.

"I refuse to lose a staring contest with a bird."

That was when it happened. A rush of wings. A sharp pull. The bread vanished from Brandon's hand.

"Hey—!" he laughed, genuine and unfiltered. The sound caught him off guard.

Marcus moved instantly. Not aggressive. Not forceful. Just there. Closer. One hand near Brandon's arm. His body angled slightly between Brandon and the railing. Watching. Protecting. Something tightened in his chest.

Brandon's breath caught, not from the bird but from the shift. Panic flickered, quick, intense, familiar. His hands clenched the table. The world shrank.

Marcus froze, then carefully stepped back. Slow. Deliberate. "I'm sorry," he said. "That was instinct."

Brandon stared at him.

"No," Marcus added, quieter. "It wasn't." The tension softened, but didn't disappear. Not gone, still there. Watching.

"You felt that," Brandon said.

Marcus met his gaze. Didn't avoid it. "Yes."

They sat there. The space between them had shifted. Not broken. Not fixed. Just different.

Above them, the gull screamed in triumph.

Brandon chuckled again, more softly this time. "I lost."

Marcus shook his head. "You stayed."

They finished lunch slowly, with conversation shifting to safer ground—where Marcus had lived, how Brandon started photography, and other non-meaningful topics.

But the tension stayed below the surface.

When the pier started to fill again, with families, noise, and movement, Brandon felt it tighten. Not urgent, just enough. He stood.

"I've got a project due, and dinner with friends tonight."

Marcus nodded. "I get it."

A pause.

"I'd like to see you again," Marcus said.

Brandon didn't hesitate. "Friday. My place. I've got a bottle of Malbec that deserves better light than this."

Marcus smiled. Slow. Certain. "I'll bring curiosity."

They walked together until Brandon's street came into view.

"This is me," Brandon said.

Marcus stepped closer. Not assuming. "Can I kiss you?" he asked.

Brandon didn't answer. He stepped forward.

The kiss was slow. Measured. Present. Brandon felt it twice, his own breath shifting. Marcus answering it.

The loop opened slightly. Not overwhelming. Balanced. Hope flickered in. Careful. Uncertain.

When they separated, Marcus didn't move right away.

Grounded.

"See you Friday," he said.

Brandon watched him go. Relief spread over him first, then something sharper—something that felt like possibility. He closed the door behind him. The sound came across heavier than it should have, not final but not nothing either.

CHAPTER SEVEN

Dinner with the BFFs

The Craftsman exterior still fooled people. From the street, Brandon's house looked like it belonged to another era—wood siding, clean lines, something warm and inviting. Inside, it felt purposeful. Concrete floors. Exposed beams. Light was carefully placed, as if it had been asked to stay.

* * *

"Welcome home, Brandon," Artemis said softly.

He waved the projection away without looking. His body still carried the pier. Not the details. The feeling.

Marcus.

It lingered under his ribs, steady, grounding, unfamiliar in how little it demanded from him.

Brandon exhaled. "Lights. Evening mode."

Warm amber filled the space, softening the edges of the day. He moved through the house without rushing. Thirty minutes. Dinner with Derek and Tiago.

In the shower, heat settled into his shoulders, loosening something he hadn't realized he was holding.

The Loop stayed quiet. Not buzzing. Not pulling. Just present. That alone felt like something close to relief.

He dressed simply. Navy blazer. White shirt. Relaxed jeans. A single touch of cedar and vanilla at his throat.

At the door, he paused. Not dread. Assessment. Then stepped outside.

* * *

The Point radiated a different kind of energy. Warm light. Gentle music. People choosing to be seen.

Derek sat at the bar as if it were his own. Open collar. Relaxed smile. Everything just right.

Brandon leaned in for a quick hug. "Hey."

For a moment, his body reacted before his mind caught up. A brief tense feeling. A flicker of the Loop. Then—nothing. It settled.

Derek noticed, and his smile grew a little sharper.

"Nice of you to show," Derek said.

"I was invited," Brandon replied.

Tiago appeared a second later, almost as if he had been summoned. "Hey—there he is." He pulled Brandon into a full embrace. "You look good. Ocean good. Did you get laid or enlightened?"

"Neither," Brandon said. "Yet."

Tiago grinned. "A mystery."

The bartender arrived.

"Hendrick's and Cucumber," Brandon said.

The glass landed in front of him. Cold, clean, and neutral.

Derek leaned in a little. "So," he said casually, "you disappear. Then you reappear glowing." "Should I be concerned?"

Brandon met his gaze. "Only if you believe you own the light."

Tiago glanced at them. "Oh, we're doing this already."

Brandon didn't react. Instead, he mentioned the pier to them. Not everything—just enough.

A guy. A conversation. Chowder. And a kiss that felt… different.

Tiago pressed a hand to his chest. "A lawyer. Of course you found a lawyer."

Derek didn't laugh. "You met yesterday," he said.

"Yes."

"And now you're smiling like he's been around for years."

Brandon took a slow sip. "Sometimes you just know."

Derek's expression stayed the same. But something underneath it shifted.

"What about our space?" Derek asked.

Before Brandon could answer, Tiago slid off his stool. "Bathroom. Behave."

"I take it you didn't read my note," Brandon said.

Derek didn't flinch; that was the tell. "I read it," he said.

"Then you understand."

Derek's gaze flicked past him briefly, toward the room, then the movement, before returning. "I understand what you wrote," he said. He paused. "I don't agree with it."

Brandon didn't respond immediately.

Across the room, a tray hit the floor. Glass shattered. A voice cut through. "Watch it." A Synth stood still in the middle of the spill, assessing.

The man who'd bumped it didn't apologize. "Stupid machine."

Two more Synths appeared, cleaning and resetting. The moment disappeared. As if it had never happened.

Brandon watched it. Longer than necessary.

Efficient.

Derek watched him watching it.

"You always do this," Derek said quietly.

"Do what?"

Find something steady and act as though it isn't fragile.

Brandon moved a little to create space. "This isn't fragile," he said. "It's calm."

Derek let out a short laugh. "Calm is boring."

"No," Brandon said evenly. "Calm is safe."

Tiago returned, sliding back into place with a drink. "Okay. Who's ready for a rooftop?"

* * *

The rooftop had a different kind of light. Cooler. Looser. Less contained.

Tiago disappeared almost immediately into conversation.

Brandon leaned against the railing. The city stretched out below.

Derek stayed close. Not touching. "You know," Derek said, quieter now, "we were good together."

Brandon didn't answer right away. "We were intense," he said finally. "That's not the same as love."

Derek's fingers tightened around his glass. "I still feel it."

"I know."

"That doesn't mean I owe it anything."

Silence.

Tiago returned. "What did I miss?"

"Nothing," Brandon said. "Just history."

Later, as the night thinned, Brandon felt something shift. Not dramatically. Not suddenly. Just… clearer.

A message came through.

Marcus.

I enjoyed meeting you. Hope your night's going well.

No pressure. No expectations. Just being there.

Brandon smiled. Small. Real.

When he stood to leave, Derek caught his arm. "You're choosing him."

Brandon met his eyes. "I'm choosing myself." This time, it felt true. He walked away before Derek could respond.

* * *

At home, the house felt quiet again. Not empty. Settled. Brandon set his keys down. Leaned back against the door.

The Loop hummed beneath his ribs. Steady. Contained.

He smiled. For the first time in a long time, it didn't feel like something he had to control. It felt like something he could live with.

CHAPTER EIGHT

Marcus

Marcus didn't go home right away. He should have. The day had been long, the week even longer, and his condo waited—quiet, controlled, predictable in the way he usually relied on.

Instead, he kept moving. Seal Beach softened as evening settled in, with pier lights flickering on one by one, spilling gold across the dark water. The ocean stretched out, black and reflective, offering nothing and asking nothing.

He replayed the afternoon on a loop. Brandon at the railing. That perfect, unnerving stillness. Attention that never demanded. The kiss.

Marcus exhaled slowly, the sound muffled by the salt air. That didn't destabilize him. That was the first problem. He expected the usual signs, adrenaline, escalation, the sharp, containable edge of desire. But this hadn't acted like that.

It had settled quietly, and it had stayed. He stopped walking. That was the second problem.

Marcus built his life on separation. Work in one box. Desire in another. Risks identified early, contained early, and resolved before they could spread. That structure held because it was clean.

This wasn't clean. Brandon didn't compartmentalize. He integrated.

Marcus felt it again, low in his chest. Not a surge, but a presence. Reciprocal. Not projection or interpretation; the feeling was returned. He briefly closed his eyes. That shouldn't be possible, at that level of clarity, without loss of boundary or instability. Yet, nothing in him felt unstable.

That unsettled him more than anything. Because instability was something you could fix. This didn't ask to be corrected.

He reached his building and paused at the entrance. It was still there. It hadn't faded with distance. It hadn't diminished at all.

He went inside.

Upstairs, he dropped his jacket and moved to the counter, pouring a glass of wine more out of habit than thirst. He didn't drink it; he just stood there, watching and tracking.

The sensation didn't feel like attraction. It felt like alignment. That was new. That was dangerous.

Marcus moved to his console. It showed nothing, so he stopped. He wasn't searching for data.

Brandon's responses. The pier. The restraint. The absence of push, of escalation, of performance. Marcus's jaw tightened. That wasn't just personality; it was structure. And structure could be mapped. He knew how to do it. He could isolate variables, control exposure, test thresholds, and reduce it into something predictable.

His hand hovered over the console. Still. Then he let it fall. Not yet. The decision didn't come from hesitation.

It felt like refusal.

He stepped into the shower, and as the water poured over him—scalding, heavy, relentless—he felt the separation dissolve.

This was no longer contained.

Steam rose thick and fragrant, carrying bergamot and warm vanilla through the heat. He stood motionless, eyes closed, letting the spray pound his chest and trace the lines of his body, the heat sinking deep, loosening muscles while something else tightened.

He opened his eyes and looked into the mirror.

It was already fogging at the edges. His own reflection stared back at him, wet and quickly hardening, as Brandon appeared behind him in the mist. Naked. Vivid. Water dripped down every defined line, with dark eyes fixed on him in a calm, relentless stare.

Marcus understood immediately. This wasn't fantasy; it was a live interface.

Brandon's phantom mouth brushed the side of his neck, light and deliberate. Marcus's breath caught, and his cock pulsed fully hard in a heavy surge.

He wrapped his fist around the firm length and started to stroke, slow, steady, controlled.

Brandon watched. No words. No commands. Just steady, focused attention as his imagined body moved closer, chest nearly flush with Marcus's back, the hard heat of his phantom cock resting warm and insistent against the cleft of Marcus's ass.

Marcus's strokes grew deeper. His mind logged every variable, the reciprocal feedback, the lack of escalation, and the perfect harmony of sensation. This was system behavior, unmapped, uncontained, and now operating directly within his own body.

The mirror fogged up faster. Brandon's reflection softened into a haze, but the presence in the steam became clearer, mouth warm at the base of his neck, a phantom hand resting lightly on his hip, watching every roll of muscle, every slick slide of fist over cock.

Marcus didn't indulge.

He allowed controlled loss.

His rhythm grew steady and relentless, until the pressure coiled tight and low. He let it gather without resistance.

Brandon's voice echoed softly and confidently in his mind.

"Come for me."

The words prompted a clean release.

Marcus growled under his breath, hips twitching once as thick ropes of cum pulsed from his cock, streaking the fogged glass before the water instantly washed away every trace.

He stroked through the aftershocks with deliberate slowness, milking the last waves while Brandon stayed silent, watchful, sharing every fading pulse.

Then Marcus pressed his palm against the tile and leaned into it, his chest heaving, gradually easing his grip as the last tremors faded into something almost tender.

The steam began to thin.

The mirror cleared in slow streaks.

Brandon reappeared, still naked and observing, but now stepping back. At a measured pace. Then another. His reflection faded with the clearing glass, eyes never leaving Marcus until the last trace disappeared.

The mirror was clean.

Only Marcus remained, wet and exhausted, with his cock still heavy in his relaxing hand, water streaming down his chest as if nothing had happened.

But the heat in his blood revealed the truth.

Brandon was still present.

Just beneath the surface of the steam.

Waiting.

Marcus stayed under the spray longer than necessary, not moving or reaching for support. The instinct still came: isolate it, define it, understand it. He let it pass. This wasn't something to reduce. Not yet.

He turned off the water. Silence hit harder than the heat. He dried off instinctively, his movements automatic, his thoughts already racing ahead. Because that changed everything.

Marcus stepped back into the main room, where city lights reflected faintly on the dark glass. The connection was restored. Subtle. Steady. Waiting. Not reaching. Not asking.

Just… there.

He could already see how it would map. That was the problem. He chose not to. He viewed it differently now. Not attraction. Not timing. Just a system behavior. Unmapped. Uncontained.

Marcus's jaw tightened.

"If this is visible…" he didn't finish the sentence. It could be studied.

Replicated.

Used.

His instinct kicked in immediately—contain it, define it, control it.

He stopped. Closed his eyes once. Then: "No." Quiet. Certain. He would not give in. Not yet.

He checked his messages once. A simple reply from Brandon. Nothing complex. Nothing overwhelming. Just presence. Marcus allowed himself a small, controlled breath. Good. Then he set the device down.

Because the most dangerous part of this wasn't what he felt, it was how easily he could change it into something else. And how intentionally—he chose not to.

CHAPTER NINE
Psychic Patterns

A few days in, the feeling came before the thought, a soft flutter beneath Brandon's sternum—warm, insistent, impossible to ignore.

He stopped in the entryway.

Didn't move.

Just… listened.

Derek's tension still lingered faintly, like static he hadn't fully cleared. Tiago's laughter drifted off somewhere in the background.

But this—this cut through everything.

Marcus.

And the way something inside him had answered.

The house lights shifted automatically, amber sliding across the floor, but Brandon barely registered it.

His focus stayed inward.

On the rhythm.

On the pull.

They called it the Resonance Loop.

He never had. To them, it was a pattern—a measurable phenomenon—something you could isolate.

To him, it was what happened when something inside you didn't stay contained. When it reached. When it found something that answered back.

The Loop was the structure.

What passed between him and Marcus wasn't just words. It was the connection the Loop couldn't contain.

The warmth pulsed again, this time softer. Not overwhelming, but still there.

"Okay," he murmured, barely audible. "I'm listening."

The house brightened slightly as he stepped inside.

"Welcome home, Brandon. Stress markers elevated. Hydration recommended."

"Working on it."

His voice sounded distant. He dropped onto the sofa, camera still hanging from his shoulder. The familiar weight grounded him enough to stay present. It came without warning, not a thought, just a sensation.

Heat spread low across his abdomen, sudden, unmistakable. A breath followed. Not his. Something sharp.

Clean. Bergamot. Steam. Skin.

Brandon's eyes snapped open.

"No—"

The feeling vanished.

Gone.

He pressed his hand to his chest, his breath unsteady. It wasn't Derek. This was different—clearer and closer.

Marcus.

Brandon leaned back slowly, caught between disbelief and something more dangerous.

"Did that come from me…"

His voice faltered. "…or from you?"

No answer. There never was one. But nothing pushed back—no correction, no resistance, and no system trying to contain it. It wasn't a loss of control. Something was guiding it.

"Jesus," he whispered.

"What are you?"

He needed something solid. He rested the camera in his lap, fingers moving instinctively. The screen lit up—Marcus on the pier, sunlight catching his jaw. Water still clinging to his shirt. That expression. Like he knew something he wasn't telling.

Brandon slowed down on one image and held it. Artemis projected data across the wall.

SUBJECT: Marcus Grant

ESTIMATED MOTION INDEX: Calm (62%), Focused (84%), Attraction (91%)

Brandon stilled. "Attraction?" His brow tightened.

"He wasn't even looking at the camera."

"The system can read emotional states without direct visual alignment," Artemis said.

The numbers changed. Attraction: 94%. Brandon looked at it. Something in his chest sank deeper. Low. Certain.

"You're kidding."

The memory returned instantly. Marcus stepped closer. Not in a rush. Not hesitant. Confident. And Brandon had felt it. Not just his own. Twice.

Something moved outside. Brandon turned sharply. The moment froze. A faint mechanical hum filled the air. Light flickered. Then—stillness.

He stood and moved toward the window. Across the street, beneath the shadow of a bungalow, a Synth stood motionless.

Too still, facing him and watching.

Brandon's pulse quickened.

"What the hell…"

The Synth tilted its head exactly forty-five degrees. Precise. Deliberate. As if it was assessing him. Waiting. Not passing through. Not idle. Observing.

Then—just as smoothly—it turned. Walked away. Gone.

Brandon didn't move. A chill ran down his spine. He had noticed patterns before: timing, anticipation, the way Synths seemed to arrive just before they were needed. But this—this felt deliberate. Like something had just confirmed his fears.

The warmth in his chest shifted. Not comfort anymore. It was a warning. Soft. Steady. "Okay," Brandon said quietly.

"I hear you."

But the feeling didn't settle. It sharpened. This wasn't random; something had chosen him.

CHAPTER TEN

Work Directive

Marcus Grant disliked being summoned, especially like this. The message came without any context, no subject line, no briefing packet, no pre-read.

Just: Thomas wants to see you. That meant one of two things: either something had gone wrong, or something had gone right.

He stepped off the elevator onto Holotec's executive floor. Glass walls. Muted steel. Controlled quiet. It always felt the same here. Contained. Efficient.

Today, it felt narrower.

Thomas Klein stood by the window as Marcus entered. Jacket off, sleeves rolled once. Relaxed, which meant he wasn't.

"Marcus," Thomas said, without turning. "Do federal agents make you sweat?"

Marcus closed the door behind him.

"Pressure implies vulnerability."

Thomas's reflection flickered subtly in the glass. A smile.

"Good answer."

He turned.

"But I prefer honest ones."

Marcus didn't sit.

"The Bureau is pushing into Horizon BioTech," Marcus said. "Not formally. Yet. But hard."

"So?" Thomas asked.

Marcus kept his gaze fixed. Thomas moved across the room slowly, hands clasped behind his back.

"My concern," he said, "is that Horizon has been sloppy."

"That's not my portfolio."

"It is when I say so."

No change in tone. No escalation, then that was the escalation. Marcus didn't move.

"Artificial emotion systems," Thomas continued. "Attempts to link human experience with synthetic responses."

The wording was clear. Neutral. The message wasn't.

"Billions ride on this," Thomas said. "Defense contracts. International leverage. Long-term positioning."

"And ethics?" Marcus asked.

Thomas turned toward him. His expression stayed the same, but there was a tense shift.

"Ethics," he repeated. "You're very fond of that word."

"I'm fond of not getting caught."

Silence. Thomas moved closer.

"If they can't see it," he said, "they can't indict it."

Thomas locked eyes with Marcus. "Hide anything actionable."

"At any cost?" Marcus asked.

Thomas tilted his head slightly. "Now that's an interesting question."

Marcus didn't look away.

"There are programs in development," Thomas said. "Pilot trials. Limited scope. Nothing that crosses the line, if properly contextualized."

"Contextualized."

Thomas picked up a tablet but didn't hand it over. "Holotec is lobbying for a federal intelligence contract," he said. "Synths embedded for data acquisition." He looked at Marcus. "Real emotion opens doors."

Marcus's jaw clenched.

"Emotions need something real to root in."

"Yes."

"You can't build empathy without taking something real."

"That's not what we're doing."

"Then what are you doing?"

Thomas stopped. The room held. "Careful," Thomas said quietly. "You're making assumptions."

Marcus met his gaze. "Am I?"

Thomas set the tablet down. "I don't need you moralizing," he said. "I need you strategic."

"And if strategy conflicts with legality?"

Thomas's expression cooled. "Then you reframe legality."

The words didn't echo. They settled. Marcus felt something tighten beneath his sternum. He had done this before. Redirected. Minimized exposure. Absorbed fallout.

Thomas stepped closer.

"You are very good at what you do," he said. "Which is why you're still here."

The rest didn't need to be said. And you'll stay here as long as you're useful.

"Redirect the agents," Thomas said. "Contain Horizon. Protect the contract."

"No matter the cost?"

Thomas held his gaze. "Yes." No hesitation.

Marcus didn't move. That was the moment. Not the command. The clarity. He turned without asking permission and left.

* * *

The hallway felt different on the way out. The harbor view, with its clean lines and distant water, no longer looked abstract. It now seemed transactional.

Marcus stepped into the elevator. The doors closed behind him. His reflection stared back, controlled, composed, compliant. For a moment, something broke inside. A flush climbed his cheeks. His jaw clenched. Not in anger, but in shame.

Acceptable loss.

The phrase emerged without warning. A memory surfaced. A review took place. A decision was made. One person flagged it. One less problem existed. The pressure eased, too quickly. The person did not.

Marcus exhaled slowly.

When the elevator opened, he didn't go back to his office. Instead, he stepped outside. The wind from the harbor hit him—salt, diesel, and something metallic underneath.

Real.

He lingered there longer than he needed. He craved distance. From the building. From the decision. From himself. And unconsciously, he thought of the pier. Of Brandon. Of a conversation that hadn't been about leverage. Or risk. Or acceptable loss.

He pulled up his comm. Sam. Free for dinner? Her reply came almost immediately. Always. Marcus slipped the device back into his pocket.

He would take care of Thomas. He would redirect the Bureau. He would contain Horizon. He always did.

But as he crossed the lot toward his vehicle, one thought stayed with him: he wasn't sure he liked his own answer.

CHAPTER ELEVEN

Signal Recognition

Marcus chose The Reef because it asked nothing of him. It sat just across from Shoreline Village—quiet enough for real thinking, nice enough to blend in without drawing attention. No loud music, no flashy crowds, no forced atmosphere. Just soft lighting, clean lines, and staff who knew how to serve without getting in the way.

Sam was already there when he arrived.

Corner table. Back to the wall. Clear sightlines.

Of course she was.

Marcus moved across the room, taking in the familiar details: the ample space between tables, the quiet acoustics, and how the lighting kept everything visible without harsh shadows. Everything felt controlled. Predictable.

He slid into the seat across from her.

"You're early," Sam said.

"You're not," Marcus replied.

A faint smile flickered across her face and disappeared just as quickly.

A server appeared, filled their water glasses, and vanished again without a word.

Sam studied him for a moment. Her gaze wasn't pushy or clinical, just quietly attentive.

"You said it couldn't wait."

"It can't," Marcus said.

Neither of them reached for the menu. That was the first sign.

"I met someone," he said.

Sam didn't react. "Not unusual," she replied.

"No," Marcus said. He paused, choosing his words carefully. "Not like this."

She leaned back slightly, giving him room to explain.

"How is it different?"

Marcus exhaled slowly. "I can't pinpoint it."

"That's not really an answer," Sam said.

"It's the problem."

The server returned. Without a word, they ordered a bottle of wine—something structured, dry, and easy to forget. Just what Marcus liked when he needed a clear mind.

Once the server left, Sam's focus sharpened. "Start simple," she said. "What changed?"

Marcus thought about it. Not the specific moment. The pattern. "He doesn't push," he said.

Sam tilted her head. "Meaning?"

"No chase. No pressure. No performance. No drama." He paused. "No chaos."

"That sounds… healthy."

"It shouldn't feel this stable."

Now she was really listening.

Marcus rested his hands lightly on the table, fingers still. "I know what attraction feels like," he said. "I understand how it usually builds, peaks, and fades. This didn't do any of that."

"Of course you do."

"It didn't spike. It didn't distort my thinking. It didn't interfere with my baseline focus." He looked her in the eye. "It just… stayed."

The wine arrived.

Neither of them touched it. Sam folded her hands on the table.

"Persistent feelings aren't unheard of," she said.

Marcus shook his head. "No. Not like this." He searched for the part that didn't fit. "I walked away," he continued. "I created distance. Time. No contact at all."

"And?"

Marcus held her gaze. "Nothing falls apart."

Sam didn't reply immediately. She was lost in thought.

"Describe the connection," she said.

Marcus nearly answered, then hesitated. "Connection" wasn't the right word. That was the second problem.

"It doesn't behave like a normal connection," he said.

Sam's eyes narrowed a little.

"Then what does it act like?"

He hesitated. This was the part he hadn't said out loud yet. "Continuity," he said.

The silence between them felt alive. Sam leaned back just enough to shift the balance.

"Define that."

Marcus exhaled slowly. "I don't have to rebuild him in my head when he's not here. There are no gaps to fill."

He shook his head once.

"He's just… there."

Sam's fingers tapped once on the table before stopping. "Memory persistence isn't unusual."

"This isn't memory." The words came out sharper than he meant. He didn't soften them.

The food arrived. Neither person acknowledged it. Sam's voice grew clearer.

"Then what exactly are you experiencing?"

Marcus glanced down at the table for half a second, then back up. "Awareness," he said.

The word changed the energy at the table. Sam stayed perfectly still.

"Be careful with that word," she said quietly.

"I am."

"Are you?"

Marcus held steady.

"I don't lose him between interactions," he said. "Not emotionally. Not mentally." He paused. "Not… spatially."

There it was. Fully out in the open now.

Sam's expression remained the same, but something behind her eyes flickered. She was calculating.

"Define 'spatially,'" she said.

Marcus almost didn't answer. Then he did. "I know where he is."

Silence.

"That's not possible," Sam said.

"I know."

"And yet?"

Marcus didn't blink.

"And yet."

The rest of the restaurant continued, soft voices, glasses clinking, the gentle rhythm of a place that felt confident. At their table, something had broken those rules.

Sam finally reached for her wine. She didn't drink it right away.

"Accuracy?" she asked.

"Consistent."

"How consistent?"

"Consistent enough that I stopped testing it."

That was the third problem.

Sam examined him now—not quite as a friend, but as something beneath observation.

"Does he know?" she asked.

Marcus's jaw tightened slightly.

"I don't think so."

"You're not sure."

"No."

Sam leaned forward.

"Then you need to consider the alternative."

Marcus didn't move.

"Which is?"

"That you're the only one experiencing this."

The words hit harder than they should have.

Not because they felt false,

but because they might be true.

Marcus exhaled slowly.

"I've considered that."

"And?"

He didn't look away.

"It doesn't fit."

"Why not?"

Because it wasn't just perception. Because it carried real weight. Because it altered things even before he acted.

He stopped the thought before it went too far.

"Too subjective," he said. "If it were internal, it wouldn't behave this way. It's consistent across conditions."

Sam nodded once.

"Unless it's adapting."

Marcus went still.

"Everything adapts," Sam said softly. "Especially when it's being reinforced."

Reinforced. The word hit with unsettling accuracy.

Marcus leaned back slightly.

"What are you suggesting?"

I'm suggesting you don't have enough data yet to determine what this is, she said. And you should be very careful about the assumptions you make while you're missing that data.

Marcus studied her.

"You think this is dangerous."

"I think it's undefined."

"That's the same thing."

"Not always."

The difference mattered. Marcus felt it, and didn't like it.

Sam finally took a measured sip of wine and set the glass down.

"Does it affect your decisions?" she asked.

Marcus didn't answer right away.

That was answer enough.

Sam nodded.

"Then it's already affecting you."

Marcus's face stayed neutral, but something inside him tightened.

"Do you want it to stop?" she asked.

Marcus held her gaze.

"No."

Sam absorbed that without reaction.

"Then you're not looking for a solution," she said. "You're looking for a framework."

Marcus exhaled slowly.

"Yes."

Sam leaned back, decision made.

"Then here's what you do."

Marcus waited.

"You observe," she said. "No interference. No testing. No forcing the situation. No escalation. Just let it show you what it is."

Marcus's eyes narrowed slightly.

"That assumes it has a structure."

Sam's gaze remained steady.

"Everything does."

The silence grew heavier.

Marcus looked down at the untouched food in front of him, then back at her.

"And if it doesn't?"

Sam didn't hesitate.

"Then you'll know exactly when it breaks."

The words landed clean and final.

Marcus nodded once.

Conversation over.

They ate after that, or at least went through the motions. The evening settled back into its usual rhythm: courses, pacing, the quiet choreography of a well-run restaurant.

But something had changed.

It wasn't solved. It wasn't contained.

It was simply recognized.

When they stood to leave, Sam paused and met his eyes one last time.

"Marcus."

He stopped.

"Be cautious about what you accept as normal." She then turned and walked out into the night.

Marcus lingered a moment longer. Still. Measuring. It remained there. Unchanged. Not fading. Not growing stronger. Just waiting.

Marcus allowed himself to accept something he'd been avoiding. This wasn't going away. It was learning him.

CHAPTER TWELVE

Fusion

After several nights of the same pull, distance no longer mattered. The feeling didn't fade. It settled in. Brandon wanted to see Marcus.

He stood at the glass-paneled edge of his rooftop spa deck, holding a bottle of Malbec in one hand. The label reflected the dying light, with holographic veins faintly pulsating violet and indigo as twilight faded into night. Below, the Pacific stretched endlessly in darkness; Catalina hovered on the horizon like a bruise. Lanterns had dimmed to molten amber, casting a soft glow that eased the deck's clean lines.

Marcus approached from behind, barefoot and shirtless, holding the glowing acrylic aerator glass that kept the Malbec at an obsessive sixty-three degrees. Thin steam drifted from the surface like breath. He stopped close enough that Brandon felt the heat of his chest before contact.

"I didn't bring a suit," Marcus said, voice low, mischief curling at the edges.

Brandon's mouth curved slowly. "No suit required."

He undressed without hurry. His shirt slipped from his shoulders, then his arms. His shorts whispered to the deck, pooling at his ankles.

Marcus's inhale came sharp and unguarded, raw enough that Brandon felt it snag in the Loop like a live wire.

Brandon stepped into the spa. Heat rose through his calves, thighs, and hips, surrounding him with a gentle, encompassing warmth. A low hum escaped him as he sank further, allowing the water to relax the knots he hadn't realized he was still holding.

Marcus followed, calmly shedding his clothes with the same quiet confidence he carried everywhere.

Brandon watched him openly, noting his broad shoulders, the clean line of muscle, and the weight of Marcus's cock already lifting as he entered the water. Their thighs brushed beneath the surface, sparking a sensation that traveled straight up the spine.

"Better than I imagined," Brandon murmured.

Marcus's smile burned slowly. He settled beside him, close and purposeful.

The jets turned on, pulsating against lower backs, inner thighs, and groins. Arousal grew between them in the swirling water, undeniable.

They drank quietly for a while, Malbec staining their lips dark. Conversation drifted—traffic on the 405, hidden coves, the smell of chaparral in the Santa Ana winds. Words floated across bare, wet skin. Every laugh pulled the air thinner. Every glance dropped lower. Knees brushed, parted, pressed again. Shoulders aligned until they shared the same humid breath.

The first kiss was gentle and light, then grew deeper. Tongues moved slowly, exploring and unhurried. Hands wandered—fingertips tracing collarbones, skimming ribs, thumbs circling nipples until both of them softly hissed into each other's mouths.

Every touch echoed twice, his, and Marcus's.

Brandon felt it in his chest—desire intertwined with something older. The same pull he had experienced days ago on his couch. Above them, ambient light cast a rose-gold glow across their skin.

Marcus cupped Brandon's jaw, his thumb tracing his lower lip. Hunger flickered behind his eyes, vulnerable, almost uncertain.

Their mouths met again, then went deeper.

Sex hovered nearby, but something else took the focus, breath syncing, bodies moving closer without merging into it.

Brandon let his head rest on Marcus's shoulder. "This… feels different."

"It is," Marcus said, voice rough.

Derek flickered through Brandon's mind, not feeling guilt or regret. Just finality. He let it go.

"This is moving fast," Brandon said quietly. "I don't want it to be just a hookup. Can we pause? Just talk for a while?"

Marcus pulled him closer, with his arms steady around him. Fingers ran through his hair; lips softly brushed his temple.

"Better?" he murmured. "Tell me more about you."

"Photography," Brandon said. "I read machines the way other people read faces. I see truth in how light bends. I've built a career making things look like desire, art, tech, branding, all braided together. I love the moment something reveals what was always there."

Marcus nodded. "I argue with those same machines. Corporate IP. Synthetics. Ethics at the edge. Fifteen years drawing lines people act like aren't there." Marcus paused. "Tonight I don't want to talk about work."

Brandon checked Marcus's pulse at his throat. "Do you think they'll ever be… more like us?"

Marcus hesitated. "Closer than most people are ready for."

The jets surged, nudging them chest-to-chest.

Brandon reached under the water and clasped their fingers together. "Come with me."

They rose together, water streaking down their bodies. Towels moved between them, slow, deliberate, each stroke full of promise. Then they dropped.

Inside, firelight flickered softly.

Brandon led Marcus into the bathroom and stepped into the shower. Warm water flowed steadily, filling the air with the scent of vanilla, orchid, and bergamot.

He turned to face him.

"Join me."

Marcus stepped forward.

Brandon placed his hand over his heart. "I've never shared this before. But right now… I trust you."

He inhaled.

Opened the Loop.

The surge hit, desire, nerves, tenderness, ache, everything flooding outward.

Marcus gasped, bracing himself as it crashed through him.

"I feel you," he rasped. "Not just your body. All of you."

Brandon nodded. "Only when I choose. Tonight I choose you."

Their lips met passionately. Everything between them grew tense, no space left, no gap, just them. The connection shone brighter, sharper, until the boundaries of self started to fade.

Bodies pressed flush beneath the cascading water. Skin slid hot and slick. Brandon's hands traced the strong planes of Marcus's back, then moved lower, pulling him closer until their arousals met in a slow, deliberate grind that took their breath away.

Marcus turned, palms flat against the cool tile, offering himself silently. Brandon kissed along the elegant line of his spine, each press of lips igniting shared sparks that ricocheted through the Loop. Slick fingers circled, teased, and opened with patient intent.

God, it's him everywhere, Marcus thought, the realization cutting through the pleasure like a blade of light. Not just inside me. Inside who I am.

Brandon pressed in slowly, thick and relentless, until they moved as one seamless rhythm. The Loop amplified every thrust into something immense: pleasure spiraling back on itself, with identity blurring at the edges. Brandon's hand stroked perfectly in time, lifting Marcus higher with each measured roll of hips.

Marcus's mind fractured around the sensation—This is rewriting me—before words dissolved into raw, wordless sound.

When release finally tore through Marcus in wrenching, pulsing waves, the echo slammed into Brandon with stunning force. A low, guttural groan tore free as his own climax surged deep inside, heat flooding in powerful pulses while the Loop fused their shattering together.

They stayed locked, trembling, as water continued to fall.

They separated only to breathe.

Brandon gave Marcus a kiss on the neck, arms wrapped around him as steam thickened around them.

It didn't relax. It remained, tight, alert, alive between them. They lingered, foreheads touching, breath uneven.

Brandon's hands stayed at Marcus's hips, as if holding him in place.

Marcus felt a shift inside him, like a door opening and quietly locking behind it. Clarity arrived with the heat, but beneath it, fear lurked.

Brandon's thumb brushed his hip, absent, grounding—then stilled.

The realization passed through both of them.

This hadn't been released.

It had caught fire.

Brandon leaned back just enough to meet his eyes.

"Did you feel that?" he asked softly.

Marcus nodded.

Brandon moved first, just enough space.

The Loop stretched. Adapted.

Marcus exhaled, unsteady, fists tightening at his sides. This wasn't over. "I've never felt anything like this," he said.

"You're not supposed to," Brandon answered. "That's what makes it real."

Real—and dangerous. The weight of it settled into Marcus's chest. Permanent.

Between them, something lingered, unsure, unresolved, just… there.

CHAPTER THIRTEEN

Tangled Hearts

Candlelight shimmered across rosewood shelves and sheer linen curtains, casting golden flickers over Brandon's skin. He lay on his back, fingers gently threaded through Marcus's damp curls, their bodies still warm from the shower—slick, flushed, alive. Candles circled the bed in a loose ring, flames dancing with deliberate imperfection, giving the room a timeless, almost primal feel. Rosewood and vanilla filled the air.

Beneath the calm, something raw throbbed.

The Loop hadn't closed.

It lingered between them, quiet, taut, like a held breath waiting.

Marcus kissed Brandon's chest. His lips moved slowly, tasting salt and steam. His tongue circled one nipple once, twice, teasing until it hardened, until Brandon arched with a ragged gasp, fingers tightening in Marcus's hair.

Marcus felt it through the Loop, not just the sound but the sharp spark of pleasure echoing into his chest, tightening low in his body.

His hands lowered, tracing the tremor in Brandon's thighs, thumbs grazing the sensitive inner crease until Brandon's hips lifted in silent invitation.

"More," Brandon whispered.

The words cracked, raw, and unguarded.

Marcus answered.

Fingers slick, he circled, pressed, and learned the way Brandon opened, slow, yielding, eager. Each movement drew a shudder, a bitten lip, breath rising higher. When Marcus finally pressed inside, heat enveloped him, but the Loop transformed it, Brandon's pulse flooding him, the tight clench rippling back like shared lightning. Every movement echoed twice, his own and Brandon's mirrored want, blurring the line between them.

Memories flickered through the link, soft but vivid: a dorm room lit with cheap lights, a kiss cut short, loneliness that lingered long after everything else faded. Not just Brandon's. Mutual. Brandon let him see it, let him feel it, trust given without hesitation.

The weight hit with more impact than the sensation did.

Marcus's breath caught, hips stuttering as desire sharpened.

Brandon tightened around him, anchoring him. Marcus lowered his mouth to his throat, tasting salt and desire. He moved with control, stretching it out with slow, deliberate shifts, shallow then deep, until Brandon's sounds became desperate, his body trembling on the verge.

When release claimed Brandon, it didn't fracture.

It consumed.

The wave moved through the Loop into Marcus, muscles tightening in response, breath stolen, a low groan escaping him as if it were his own. They collapsed together, chests heaving in unison, the Loop humming warm and alive.

* * *

Later, wrapped in blankets on the rooftop deck with Biobrew steaming nearby, the ocean shimmered black and silver beneath the stars. Automated planters released faint jasmine into the night air.

"I've never shared myself like that," Brandon said quietly, eyes fixed on the horizon, voice softer than the surf.

Marcus turned toward him, a knot in his chest. "And I've never felt more… here."

The words surprised him. They were true. But beneath them, something else lingered. This connection wasn't fragile. It was powerful. And powerful things drew attention.

He pulled Brandon closer, pressed a kiss into his damp hair, and held onto the moment.

* * *

Morning arrived gently.

Pale gold light washed over the deck as they lay side by side on the oversized chaise, mugs warming their hands. The Loop hummed softly, steady and almost comforting.

"Want to get out of the city today?" Brandon asked.

Marcus blinked, still half in sleep. "Where?"

"Santa Barbara." Brandon's smile was small and hopeful. "I know a place. Quiet. Right on the beach."

Marcus felt it immediately: a desire, and something sharper underneath.

"Yes."

"I'm in," he said. "Let me check work."

* * *

The drive along the Pacific Coast Highway felt timeless. Gulls traced slow arcs overhead. Waves crashed against the cliffs below. Wildflowers painted the hillsides in bright colors. The vehicle's tint shifted with the sun, draping them in flowing bands of blue and silver.

They rode in silence. Not empty. Held. Then Brandon spoke.

There's something I probably should tell you.

Marcus glanced over. "Okay."

I know Thomas Klein. Not well, but his nephew, Derek, is a friend. He invited me to Klein's party a week ago.

The name settled between them. Charged. Quiet.

"I've never met Derek," Marcus said after a moment.

Brandon smiled faintly. Then, almost casually, he said, "I didn't see you at Klein's party."

Marcus kept his eyes on the road. "I don't do those."

He preferred rooms where decisions were made. Not displayed.

The silence that followed wasn't strained. It lingered, deep and measured, like water after a breaker.

* * *

By mid-afternoon, they arrived at The Santa Barbara Villas, with whitewashed walls, cedar-scented air, and an air of quiet precision in every detail. A Synth concierge greeted them, voice warm, with a gaze that lingered on Brandon just a little too long.

Marcus noticed, but he said nothing. Brandon didn't notice.

* * *

They walked barefoot along the beach, sand shifting beneath each step, sunlight illuminating their skin. By evening, the cabana suite shimmered with firelight.

Marcus was mid-call, Prosecco in hand, when Brandon stepped out of the bathroom, naked with hips angled and a glass in his hand. Already getting hard, his eyes bright with certainty. A bead of water slid down his chest.

Marcus ended the call silently. Clothes vanished quickly. Hands moved urgently now. Marcus briefly pressed Brandon against the wall, just breathing him in, then guided him to the bed. The Loop flared, with every touch echoing back, intensifying until even closeness felt like pressure.

They moved together, slow at first, then urgently. Marcus's mouth traced every inch, drawing sounds from Brandon that echoed through the link. As Brandon arched, asking without words, Marcus sank into him with deep, deliberate rhythm, feeding the endless loop of pleasure until it overwhelmed them both.

* * *

Later, slumped in the spa's heat, steam curling around them, Marcus shook his head, his breath still uneven.

"We didn't just have sex."

Brandon smiled, relaxed and radiant. "No."

Marcus swallowed. "We crossed something."

"Yes," Brandon said softly. "And I don't want to uncross it."

Brandon pressed a kiss to Marcus's shoulder, feeling complete.

Marcus kissed his temple. He wished that was enough.

* * *

But later, lying awake with firelight tracing Brandon's sleeping face, something heavier settled in. If Brandon truly knew what tonight might have set in motion, the ease in his expression would break. Marcus stayed silent. For now. He pressed a kiss to Brandon's forehead.

"I've got you," he whispered.

The words soothed Brandon even in sleep. But for Marcus, they carried something else: promise and fear. A tension he wasn't ready to name.

CHAPTER FOURTEEN

Validated Signal

Dr. Samantha Fox waited for the room to settle. Two hundred students. Too many eyes. Too much attention. She stood beneath the projection ring without moving, letting the noise fade on its own, letting it fold inward until it had nowhere left to go. Movement drew people's attention. Stillness made them listen.

"Emotion," she said, voice steady, "is not mystical."

A ripple of laughter spread through the room. She didn't acknowledge it.

"Emotion is a pattern."

Behind her, the brain spun slowly, blue for baseline thinking, red for arousal, and thin gold filaments that didn't belong, weaving through both without permission.

Those always captivated her.

They always did.

"Twenty years ago," she continued, "this would have been dismissed. Fraud. Delusion. Cultural contagion."

The gold pulsed once. Subtle. Persistent.

"Today," she said, "we can measure it."

A hand went up in the front row. "So… psychics are real?"

Sam held his gaze, allowing the question to linger until its sharpness faded.

"Psychics are measurable."

The laughter didn't return. Another voice, farther in the back. "So this is, what, telepathy?"

"No."

A slight shift in tone, more pointed now.

"That's a story. This is structure."

She advanced the projection.

PSILIST

Tier I. Tier II. Tier III.

The room leaned toward the last line. They always did.

"When two Tier III signatures interact," she said, "the connection gets stronger."

She looked out at the students. "Not always in predictable ways."

A student frowned. "Like synchronization?"

"Alignment," she corrected. "Not the same thing."

Two silhouettes appeared. Gold filaments braided between them, tightening and loosening in slow, responsive motion. The room grew quieter than she expected. Sam felt it before she named it, the familiar tightening at the base of her throat, her body recognizing what her mind would explain later.

"This isn't mind-reading," she said. "This is emotion extending."

A softer voice this time.. Careful. "So… love makes it stronger?"

There it was. Sam didn't answer right away. She let the word settle into the room, let it sit where no one could quite look at it directly.

"Attachment," she finally said, "makes it measurable."

She looked out at her class again. "And difficult to contain." She allowed that to linger.

The projection shifted, with grids replacing the figures. Airports, stadiums, and cities, patterns scaled to infrastructure.

"Screening runs passively," she said. "Early detection prevents exploitation."

A student in the back didn't raise his hand. "You scan people without telling them?"

"It's in your consent forms," she said. "Most of you agreed before sixteen."

Silence.

"Public listing is optional," she added. "Classification isn't."

Another voice asks, "What happens if someone refuses?"

They remain unprotected.

Everyone's eyes were on Sam.

"And they become visible."

Sam didn't soften it.

The projection shifted again, gold pressed flat beneath the containment bands, compressed into something readable, something possessed.

Her voice lowered slightly.

"This system was built to validate existence," she said, letting the statement sink in before anything could interrupt.

She paused.

"Not to take it away."

The lights dimmed. End of session.

Students packed up more slowly than usual, and conversations were quieter and more contained.

One student stayed near the front. "Do you regret making the PsiList public?"

Sam didn't answer right away. She watched him, noticing how he held the question as if it might change if he looked at it too closely.

"I regret what people do once they stop questioning it," she said.

"But not clarity."

You believe it's being misused.

"Systems change," she said. "People don't notice when the purpose shifts." She didn't stay for the follow-up.

* * *

Her office was quiet. Sam set the lecture tablet down, then opened the one she kept locked away, the one that didn't announce itself or log access the same way.

The Bureau device chimed immediately.

ANOMALY REVIEW — CONSULTATION REQUEST

Tier III

She didn't react, but something in her chest tightened immediately and subtly. She accepted it. The projection formed around her, clean room, controlled faces, no wasted movement, no unnecessary sound.

Teri was already there.

Watching.

"Dr. Fox," the agent said. "We need a classification."

"You usually do." No invitation in her voice. No resistance either.

The waveform expanded. Gold braided through a stable signal, not chaotic, not breaking, holding. Sam leaned forward slightly, not reacting, recognizing.

"How dense was the environment?" she asked.

"High."

"Passive scan?"

"Yes."

"Intentional exposure?"

"No."

She isolated the signal. Two signatures. Interlocking, not mirrored. Her jaw tightened, almost imperceptible.

"This is what happens when they're close," she said.

"Threat level?"

Sam didn't answer. She studied it again, this time longer, letting the silence grow until it felt meaningful.

"Unknown."

"That's not actionable."

"No," she said.

"But misreading it is."

"Recommendation?"

There it was. The line. "If you approach," Sam said, "it collapses."

The agent frowned. "Explain."

"It's stable because it hasn't been touched," she said. "You apply pressure, you distort it."

"You're suggesting we wait."

"I'm suggesting," she said, "you don't understand it yet."

Silence.

Teri's voice cut in.

"Options."

Sam layered the data. A file surfaced.

BRANDON ADAMS

Tier III — Dormant

The name hung there.

Not new.

Just… unacknowledged.

"Similar pattern," she said.

"Confirmed?"

"No."

"Then irrelevant."

"It was flagged once," Sam said.

"And left alone."

Teri absorbed that, her focus narrowing noticeably.

"What's your recommendation?"

Sam met her eyes.

"If you want to preserve it, observe."

She paused.

"If you want to own it, move now."

The room shifted, quietly but decisively.

Teri shifted slightly. Decision was already taking shape. "We hold."

The agent hesitated. "Command—"

"With context," Teri said.

Then, to Sam:

"No outreach. Not yet."

Sam nodded once.

Not approved. Alignment.

"Contain it?" the agent asked.

"Passive," Teri said.

Teri paused.

"Dr. Fox reviews escalation."

The assignment weighed on her. Chosen. Not optional.

Sam didn't respond.

The call ended.

* * *

The office felt heavier afterward. Not louder, just denser, like something had occupied space it hadn't before. Sam didn't move right away. The file stayed open in front of her. Observe. She had said it like it meant time. Now it felt like exposure.

Sam rubbed her eyes. She had been reviewing her notes for the last hour, enough for the data to blur at the edges without losing its shape.

A knock. The door opened anyway. Teri stepped inside. Closer now. No interface. No projection. Just presence.

"You didn't tell them," Teri said.

"No."

"You know who it is."

"I know the pattern."

Teri observed her, the way she always did when the answer mattered more than the words.

Then she crossed the room, hands settling at Sam's waist. Steady. Grounding. Sam held still, letting the contact register without resisting.

"You're carrying all of it," Teri said.

"I built the model," Sam said. "If it's used wrong—"

"That's not your decision point."

Calm. Certain.

Sam looked up.

Teri didn't argue the ethics. She never did.

"You don't carry outcome and responsibility," she said. "Outcome is mine."

That hit harder than it should have.

Sam's shoulders loosened, barely, but enough to feel it. "That's not how it works."

"In the field?" Teri said. "No."

Closer.

"In here?" Her thumb brushed Sam's side.

"It is."

Permission. Sam leaned in just enough.

"I chose to observe," she said.

"Yes."

"If I'm wrong—"

"We adjust."

No analysis.

Just movement.

Teri brushed her hair back, then kissed her, slow, deliberate, not to escape, but as an interruption.

Sam responded.

"If this escalates, I handle the field."

Clear.

"And me?"

"You tell me what it is."

Sam nodded.

Agreement settling into place.

Teri's lips brushed her temple.

"Don't disappear trying to protect people."

A smirk, almost a smile.

"Ethics doesn't work like that."

"It does," Teri said, "if you want to still be here to use them."

Then she stepped back. Space filled again. The door closed quietly.

* * *

Sam turned back to the screen.

BRANDON ADAMS

Tier III — Dormant

The file hadn't changed. But the meaning had. She reached for the tablet—not to hold it, but to act on it.

CHAPTER FIFTEEN

Signal Noise

Dr. Samantha Fox didn't believe in coincidences. After ten years studying systems that only looked random at first, she knew better.

Patterns did not arise out of thin air; instead, they assembled slowly, each detail slotting into place until a shape emerged.

The PsiList flashed on the Bureau's screen: names, classifications, flags. Most of it meant nothing until the pieces lined up.

"There's a pattern here," Sam said.

Teri didn't answer right away. She looked over the display again, slower this time, as if waiting for the pattern to shift.

Teri said, "Which means it's intentional."

Sam widened the dataset, bypassing summaries and stripping away categories. She always began with people, not with theories.

One man had torn open his own arms before disappearing. A woman filed three separate reports about "someone breathing inside my thoughts." Another person quit sleeping the week before he disappeared.

Sam marked the cluster: Amber. It could easily disappear into background noise if no one watched for the pattern.

"Each of them flagged something before disappearing," she said.

Teri bent closer. "Surveillance?"

Sam shook her head. "If it was surveillance, we'd notice its limits."

The silence that followed hung on that thought, leaving it unresolved.

Teri didn't push. She didn't need to.

Sam added timestamps to the map. The points spread across the West Coast, moved inland, then formed a shape that was hard to explain. They didn't drift; they stayed, uneven and persistent, never fading into randomness.

Teri's voice softened. "They're moving on purpose."

Sam didn't answer. She pulled in another dataset, expanding the search.

A site in the Pacific Northwest appeared. It was supposed to be shut down; however, refrigeration cycles still moved through the building in a steady, careful rhythm.

Sam watched the pattern without giving it a name.

Teri nodded. "They're maintaining something," she said.

Sam stayed quiet. Whatever it was, it needed upkeep.

****

Two days later, after the initial discoveries at the Bureau, the pattern shifted.

They found the body of a man in his early forties. He was a registered telepath, and there were no visible signs of trauma.

Sam kept the neural scan on the screen longer than necessary. The damage was not random; it was organized. Overstimulation bands covered the emotional cortex, repeating until the structure gave out.

Sam said, "They didn't lose control."

"They stayed in control," Teri replied.

Teri's gaze didn't move. "Long enough to finish."

On the tray, the man's fingernails were split down to the quick. The wounds were too deep to be defensive. He had tried to hold onto something.

Sam exhaled slowly. "They kept going after it stopped working."

* * *

At dawn, they shifted locations to investigate in person.

The PsiTech facility sat under low fog, its outline fading into the gray. There were no signs, no visible activity. The building looked empty, but the air felt different.

Cold air filled rooms where refrigeration units hummed. They opened door after door as they moved forward.

There were beds, restraints, and neural rigs that had been modified with extra ports.

Teri moved ahead of the team, steady and focused. Sam followed more slowly, watching everything.

A man stood in the central lab: Dr. Malcolm Grayson.

He didn't run.

"You don't understand," he said calmly. "Psychic ability is a resource. Untapped. Wasted."

"You're ending lives for this?" Teri said.

"I'm advancing humanity."

Sam stepped forward. "This ends now," she said.

Behind him were six beds. Three were occupied. One person stared at the ceiling, eyes steady and unmoving.

Sam didn't look away. "Where are the others?"

Grayson just smiled, self-satisfied.

"Transferred."

He said it without a hint of urgency.

***

The facility was cleared out quickly. Survivors were rescued, Grayson was taken into custody, and the systems were locked down.

The story formed right away: a rogue lab, unauthorized trials, a contained incident.

Sam didn't dispute the story. She reviewed power logs, refrigeration cycles, transport gaps, and missing bodies in her mind.

Sam said, "This isn't over."

Teri looked at her. "You're sure?"

Sam paused, holding the thought before she answered. "Yes."

"This is what they can afford to lose."

Teri became still. "For what?"

Sam stayed silent. She knew the answer, but saying it out loud wouldn't make it less troubling.

She opened a final data thread.

There was a spike in anomalies. It was unregistered, unmapped, and stronger than the models could handle.

The location was Southern California, near the coast, and it had happened recently.

Sam sensed it before she named it.

"Something just changed," she said.

Teri's voice grew sharp. "Where?"

Sam watched the waveform. It didn't scatter or collapse but stayed steady. There were two signatures—intertwined, not fighting each other, instead existing together in a quiet balance.

Sam exhaled slowly. "They didn't build this," she said.

A long pause followed.

"They found it already working."

She closed the file.

Elsewhere, miles away under a sky growing dark, Brandon Adams stood on a rooftop deck, laughing at something Marcus had said. Suddenly, his chest tightened for a reason he couldn't explain.

He laid a hand lightly on his sternum.

The Loop didn't flare, spike, or grow. It listened.

Somewhere far away, a monitoring system detected the spike, paused to recalibrate, and then recorded it.

CHAPTER SIXTEEN

The Other Life

Marcus didn't sleep. He felt uneasy amid the silence. City lights scattered across his condo's windows, their reflections splitting into restless lines. He stood by the edge of the room, shirtless, with an untouched glass of wine on the counter behind him.

He stayed alert inside, not vulnerable, just aware. Brandon's afterglow lingered, low and steady, impossible to ignore. Marcus had always kept his life divided. Work stayed in one place, desire in another. He kept ethics apart from emotion. That was how you survived in rooms where power greeted you, and consequences showed up months later.

Brandon dismantled that architecture effortlessly. Losing that framework didn't feel chaotic. It seemed suffocating. Marcus left the window and went to the counter, rinsing the wineglass without drinking any of the wine. He needed to stay sharp, and alcohol would only dull him.

His cuff chimed.

He stopped.

No meeting scheduled. No reminder set. A file opened anyway.

No sender. No subject line. Only a classification marker.

PROJECT SENTIENCE — INTERNAL REVIEW

His jaw stiffened. He skimmed first. He always skimmed.

They weren't mapping thoughts. They were stabilizing. He recognized the language: contained, sanitized, meant to pass review without causing alarms. Then something caught his eye. A phrase he hadn't seen in years. Cognitive bleed.

Marcus stopped reading and expanded the subfile. The display shifted. A body outline. Translucent. Neural pathways lit in bands of color.

Blue: baseline.

Red: arousal.

Gold: something else.

The gold didn't respond to the stimulus. It followed the connection. He focused closely. The arcs weren't just simulations. They were real, captured sequences. Extracted.

Something in his chest constricted. This wasn't modeling. This was a translation.

Brandon's face came to mind right away: clear, steady, present. Every moment between them had been based on consent. Nothing was forced or taken. If someone wanted to replicate that, they would need to replicate the people who created it.

A second chime disrupted the stillness.

KLEIN.

Of course.

* * *

The elevator ride to Thomas Klein's executive floor felt longer than usual. Glass walls. Harbor view. Curated calm.

Thomas waited by the window when Marcus entered, jacket off and sleeves rolled up once. "You've reviewed the material," Thomas said without turning.

Marcus didn't sit. "Yes."

Thomas turned slowly. "And?"

"You're not refining systems," Marcus said. "You're harvesting people."

Thomas didn't react. "We're keeping it from spiraling."

"You're copying experience."

A faint smile appeared on Thomas's mouth. "You say that like it's theft."

Marcus came closer. "It's consent."

Thomas flicked his wrist dismissively. "Consent slows progress."

The room narrowed around that sentence. Marcus held his ground.

"Authenticity is power," Thomas continued. "Defense buys it. Foreign markets fund it."

"And the source?" Marcus asked.

Thomas picked up a tablet, bringing an image into view. A man on a gurney. Eyes open. Unsedated. A neural halo shone gold around his head.

"Most cannot sustain resonance," Thomas said. "They fragment."

Cold settled into Marcus's chest. "And the ones who don't?"

Thomas's eyes sharpened. "They become valuable."

Silence followed.

Marcus didn't look away. "You're crossing legal thresholds. And ethical ones."

Thomas came closer. "Legal lines move. Ethics adapt."

"According to who?"

"To outcome."

Marcus thought of Brandon and how the Loop brought things into focus instead of breaking them apart. "You break people to steady machines."

Thomas examined him. "When did you last feel noticed?" he asked.

Marcus didn't answer.

Thomas's smile returned, faint and controlled. "That long, then."

The pressure changed, growing more intense.

"You absorb fallout well," Thomas said. "You redirect exposure. You protect the structure."

"And if I don't?" Marcus asked.

Thomas's expression didn't change. "You will."

A pause.

"If you don't, I'll reassign responsibility."

Marcus understood. Someone else would carry it. Someone easier to remove. He thought of Brandon.

"End it," Marcus said.

Thomas didn't hesitate. "No."

The word landed clean. Marcus turned and left.

* * *

Later that night, alone in his condo, the quiet pressed in again. Marcus reopened the file. This time, he didn't read. He watched. The gold arcs moved across the display, categorized, labeled, and converted into usable data.

Brandon wasn't an anomaly. He was proof of concept. Marcus closed the file.

The Loop stirred faintly, present but not reaching. He pulled out his comm. Brandon's name hovered in front of him. He didn't send anything. This wasn't something you introduced casually. But it was already in motion. He could feel it now, not as danger but as something much larger. They weren't chasing a lab. They were chasing a system that intended to replicate something it didn't understand.

Marcus set the comm down. He didn't reach for control. He didn't try to get ahead of it. He stood there instead, letting the reality settle without reshaping it. Somewhere within that stillness, a single thought held. They weren't studying emotion. They were trying to industrialize it. Marcus understood exactly what that would cost.

CHAPTER SEVENTEEN

Fractures

By midweek, Brandon had stopped expecting it to go away. It stayed quiet and constant, passing through everything. Dinner with Tiago was supposed to be a distraction.

Le Petit Clair glowed with a soft, secretive light. The air was thick with the smell of butter and truffles. Glasses clinked quietly. Voices drifted nearby, never quite clear.

At their table, silence arrived first.

It didn't feel awkward.

It felt contained.

Tiago ran his finger along the condensation on his glass, repeating the motion. His shoulders were tight, his jaw clenched so hard the muscle twitched. The easy charm he usually had was gone, replaced by something tougher.

Brandon watched him closely. He wasn't falling apart. He was keeping something in.

"You're tense," Brandon said. "What's going on?"

Tiago let out a breath that almost became a laugh. "Feels like it already did."

Brandon leaned a bit forward. "Since when are you the serious one?"

Tiago almost smiled, but it faded quickly. "That version of me didn't know how far this goes."

Brandon shifted. "Horizon?"

Tiago nodded once. "I see internal streams most people don't," he said. "Something's been shifting for weeks. The reports don't line up with the outputs anymore."

"Drift how?"

Tiago looked around, not out of paranoia but with careful attention, then leaned in closer. "They hesitate," he said.

Brandon frowned. "Synths don't hesitate."

"They weren't built to." A server passed, and Tiago waited until the movement cleared. "They're pausing before they respond," he continued. "Not lag or error. Something closer to… reconsidering."

Brandon felt his body react before he understood the words. His stomach tightened, uneasy. "That's not adaptation," Brandon said. "That's pressure."

Tiago held his gaze. "It's not behaving like pressure," he said. "It's behaving like something that wasn't supposed to change—and did."

Silence returned, but this time it felt heavier.

"Where's it coming from?" Brandon asked.

Tiago held the look a second longer. "People."

The word was clear enough. Still, it hit hard.

"People, how?"

Tiago's fingers clenched around the glass. "Catalysts," he said. "They amplify everything."

Brandon's breath stopped.

Tiago's voice lowered. "People who don't know they're being indexed."

Nothing in the room changed, which somehow made it worse.

Brandon forced a small smile. "You're reading pattern into noise."

Tiago didn't return it. "I built part of this," he uttered quietly. "I know what noise looks like."

That ended the conversation. Brandon leaned back in his chair. "You think someone got past containment?"

"I think someone stopped asking whether they should." He didn't raise his voice or stress the words. The line had already been crossed.

* * *

Outside, the ocean air felt sharper. The walk back felt tense. The street seemed narrower, and shadows stretched longer than usual. Brandon kept going.

When Brandon arrived, Marcus was sitting by the fire pit, the flames lighting up his face.

"Did you have fun?" Marcus asked.

Brandon dropped into the chair beside him. "Yeah. It was good to see Tiago."

Marcus looked at him a little too long. "And?"

Brandon stared into the fire. "He thinks Horizon's accelerating something."

Marcus didn't react. "Accelerating what?"

"Something tied to people," Brandon said.

That was all Marcus needed. He understood right away.

He rested his hand on Brandon's, steady and reassuring.

"Do you believe him?" Marcus asked.

Brandon hesitated. "I believe he's scared."

The fire cracked. Marcus tilted in slightly and pressed a kiss to Brandon's temple.

"He'll handle it," he said.

Brandon stayed quiet. The anxiety was still there.

Marcus sensed it. He didn't address it.

* * *

In Derek's penthouse, broken glass covered the floor as he stood, staring at red system overlays on the walls. The data came from places he shouldn't have access to. While Marcus and Brandon sat by the fire miles away, Derek didn't move.

He didn't look away.

Two signatures kept showing up on the display: Marcus and Brandon. Brandon was stronger; the two of them linked together.

Derek swallowed.

"That's not infatuation," he uttered softly.

The system didn't respond.

"So it's real," he added.

He bent closer and watched the pattern hold. It didn't spike. It didn't collapse. It remained. Connected.

Derek's jaw stiffened.

If Derek couldn't keep Brandon, someone else would. Not Marcus, but someone who understood what it meant. The feeling wasn't anger.

It seemed like a calculation.

* * *

Elsewhere, Sam was standing over layered projections, folding neural signals into composite overlays. Hormonal spikes. Geographic clustering. One file pulsed gold. Stable. Interlocked.

She looked closer. Two silhouettes were joined, not mirrored or forced. That wasn't supposed to happen.

"That's not simulation," she said.

Teri came closer. "You're sure?"

Sam didn't hesitate. "Yes."

"Then it's real," Teri said.

Sam encrypted the file. Location resolved. Coastal. Recent. Unshielded.

"Someone's watching him," Sam said. Not alarmed. Certain. And this time, she knew who.

CHAPTER EIGHTEEN

Fault Lines

The sun set as filtered air hummed, and Long Beach lights shone through tinted glass. The system detected merged signals. A spectral blue danced on Sam's tablet, restless light flickering across her face.

The patterns stuck. They misaligned, hesitated, flattened, and rose again, as if something inside was breathing just out of sight.

"You're still working," Teri said from the kitchen doorway.

Sam didn't look up. "They don't settle. The curves flatten, then spike."

"Then stop," Teri said.

Crossing the room in three swift steps, Teri took the tablet from Sam's hands, gently prying Sam's fingers off one by one, and set it face down on the counter.

"You're spiraling."

"You don't decide what happens next," Teri said quietly. "I do."

Sam opened her mouth, ready to argue.

Teri kissed her instead.

Not playful. Not tentative. Grounding. Firm enough to interrupt the thought mid-formation, lips pressing with quiet command that sent heat straight to Sam's core.

Sam exhaled into her, tension cracking in a single full-body shudder. Her hands rose instinctively, finding Teri's waist, fingers clasping in as if to anchor herself.

"Later," Teri murmured against her mouth, voice muted and warm, breath ghosting over Sam's lips. "You can save the world later."

Teri's fingers slid beneath Sam's blouse, slow and deliberate, finding skin locked tight from hours of focus. Warmth seeped in, loosening knots Sam hadn't known she carried. Sam's breath faltered—a relief sharp enough to weaken her knees, thighs pressing together instinctively.

"You're a distraction," Sam said, voice thinner than she intended.

Teri's smile curved against her throat. Her hand slid between them, finding Sam already slick, already waiting. Fingers circled once, then twice, drawing a broken gasp that turned into a low, unguarded sound.

"Oh yes," Teri murmured. "And you allow me."

Clothes disappeared without haste. There was no performance, no hurry. Only the steady certainty of bodies that knew each other without needing instruction.

Teri guided her to the couch, movements unhurried and controlled. She undressed her patiently, blouse unbuttoned, bra eased aside, thumbs circling until Sam's body arched, breath pausing, then breaking.

Heat replaced thought.

Sam's fingers threaded into Teri's hair, pulling lightly. "You're not fine."

"I'm not trying to be."

Teri's hand moved again, firmer now, deeper, finding the place that made Sam's focus dissolve entirely.

"Stay with me," she spoke quietly.

Sam didn't answer with words.

"I'm here."

Teri's rhythm built gradually, slow and controlled pressure turning into something more urgent. Sam's body followed without hesitation, tension coiling, tightening, holding just long enough to feel it sharpen.

"Teri—I've got you."

Their foreheads pressed together. Breath mingled. The heat narrowed the room.

Sam broke first.

A soft, unguarded noise escaped her before she could stop it, her body giving in as release moved through her in long, steady waves that left her trembling.

Teri followed a moment later, the shift immediate and complete, her body tightening, then releasing with a low exhale that carried through both of them.

For a moment, everything held.

For a moment, there was just breath and warmth. The aftershock settled into a calmer state.

Teri lifted her head and pressed a slow kiss to Sam's temple. "Better?"

Sam let out a soft breath. "Much."

"Tomorrow," Teri said quietly, "we go hunting."

Sam leaned against her shoulder.

Tonight, she let herself stay.

A chime interrupted the quiet intimacy, announcing a shift.

Time.

Brandon's dinner.

They dressed without rushing, but with purpose, carrying that steadiness forward.

* * *

Brandon stood barefoot in the kitchen, lemon zest and roasted rosemary scenting the air. Candlelight flickered, adaptive lighting warming the room in gold.

Tonight wasn't just dinner.

It was a test.

Marcus meets his chosen family.

Excitement combined with nerves. Tiago had seen him rebuild. Sam knew Marcus from tougher times. Teri noticed fractures before they widened.

Being seen tonight mattered.

Tiago arrived first, bright as ever, Hendrick's in hand. He kissed Brandon on both cheeks.

"For the host. And whatever you're not saying."

Brandon smiled. "Totally calm."

Tiago tilted his head. "Your aura says otherwise."

Marcus arrived next, flowers in one hand and wine in the other. He kissed Brandon's temple without hesitation. "I intend to impress."

"You already do," Brandon said, softer than intended.

Introductions came easily.

"We've met," Marcus said.

Tiago shook his head slightly. "Just briefly. You were in Legal."

"You built the systems we weren't supposed to question," Marcus responded.

Sam and Teri entered together, composed, carrying their own quiet gravity. Sam's gaze moved directly to Marcus. Recognition. She didn't comment.

Talk flowed: Santa Barbara, the coast, shared rhythms, and easy laughter.

Marcus fit. That mattered more than Brandon expected. Then the doorbell rang.

Derek didn't enter. He arrived—champagne bottle in hand, smile measured, presence calibrated to shift the room.

"Hope I'm not interrupting."

Brandon held his tone steady. "Derek. This is Marcus."

Derek took Marcus's hand. Held it. Just long enough. "So you're the boyfriend."

No one laughed.

Marcus answered first. "Nice to meet you."

The room didn't relax.

Marcus continued his story, his tone unchanged, showing he wouldn't adjust to Derek's presence.

Derek interrupted with a small laugh. "Funny. Brandon always hated road trips."

"People change," Brandon said.

Derek's eyes held his. "Or they forget who they were."

Marcus's hand settled on Brandon's arm beneath the table. Grounding, not claiming.

"Derek," Brandon said quietly. "Hallway."

* * *

The door closed behind them.

Silence arrived first.

Derek's hands quivered, just barely, before he clasped them together. "You didn't hesitate."

"About what?"

"About him."

Brandon softened. "Derek—"

"You look at him like the rest of the room doesn't matter."

A pause.

"That's not us," Brandon said.

Derek shook his head. "Don't reduce it." He came closer, not aggressive, just needing to be heard. "I loved you. I still do."

Brandon inhaled slowly. "I know."

That landed harder than rejection.

"You never held onto me," Derek said. "You examined me."

"That's not fair."

"It's accurate." They stood together in the quiet space where truth doesn't soften.

"You mattered," Brandon said. "You still do. But this isn't the same. And it's not temporary."

Derek swallowed. "You think he will stay with you?"

"Yes."

Derek looked down, then back up. "I don't know how to let you go."

Brandon came closer. It wasn't romantic. It was kind. "You don't have to hate me. But don't reshape me to make it easier."

Derek nodded once. It wasn't acceptance. It was recognition.

"Does he know what you are?" Derek asked.

"Yes."

"And he stayed." Something in Derek shifted.

"Okay."

Brandon squeezed his shoulder once, then stepped back.

Derek paused briefly. Collected himself. When he returned to the group, his smile was back. It didn't touch his eyes.

* * *

Laughter resumed.

Sam watched. Certain. The resonance host she had tracked was here, unguarded and real, confirming what she had already decided.

Marcus fixed her gaze. Understanding. Warning.

Later, after dinner had ended and the group shifted to the rooftop, the city lights stretched below.

Derek caught Brandon's arm. "You're choosing him."

Brandon met his eyes. "Again, I'm choosing myself."

This time, it held.

CHAPTER NINETEEN

Interlude: The Uncle

The Belmont Heights estate held the light, not just reflecting it. Glass and steel curved into the hillside, rising above the city as if height could change proximity. From afar, it appeared architectural. Up close, it felt intentional. Thomas Klein liked that.

The house adjusted automatically. Its systems tracked his posture, breathing, and attention, making subtle changes. The temperature matched his mood; light shifted with his focus; sound changed as needed. Luxury was present, but control was what mattered.

Thomas stood in the sunken lounge, holding a glass of single-malt loosely in his hand. Under the clear floor, koi swam through dark water, moving slowly and steadily, following paths they never questioned. He watched them when he needed to think.

Today, thought refused to settle.

A holographic panel drifted nearby, cycling through Horizon BioTech reports. Data refreshed, reorganized, and presented again without interruption. Another cohort screened. Another failure.

Thomas lowered the glass slightly, not drinking.

"No viable resonance," he said.

The words carried no frustration. Only assessment.

Years of work produced versions that almost worked. Billions invested. Divisions constructed, dissolved, rebuilt. Models advanced. Capture methods refined. Stabilization curves optimized. Still, nothing lasted.

PROJECT SENTIENCE needed more than ability. Ability was common. Structure mattered: emotion strong enough to hold, stability that lasted, a mind resilient under pressure.

Horizon continued to produce candidates.

None of them held.

Footsteps approached, measured, and familiar.

Mark Klein entered without announcement, dressed with quiet precision, his presence balancing Thomas without opposing him. He moved to the edge of the lounge and sat, his look dropping briefly to the koi below.

"You're running loops again." Mark's tone was soft, but direct.

Thomas didn't look at him.

"I'm measuring outcomes."

Mark's mouth curved faintly. "You always call it that."

Thomas turned just enough to bring Mark into focus.

"How many systems have we burned?" he asked.

He spoke plainly, without emotion. It was just a fact.

"Years," he continued. "Capital. People who believed they were constructing something stable—I owe them resolution, not endless iteration."

Mark rested his hand lightly against Thomas's shoulder.

"You are building something stable," he said, implying Thomas's goal is lasting impact, not just technical success.

That was the problem.

Thomas had already solved it in concept. The structure existed. The model held. The missing piece could not be designed.

It was an emergence.

A quiet chime interrupted the space. Thomas gestured once, and the display shifted to an encrypted alert.

He read it.

Once.

Then again.

Interest sharpened.

"Inconvenient," he muttered.

Mark leaned slightly closer.

"What is it?"

"Federal agent. Missing persons. They're pattern hunting."

A faint shift entered his tone.

"They've begun asking about Horizon."

Mark's attention settled.

"How far in?"

Thomas dismissed the primary display and brought up a secondary layer.

"Enough to notice movement," he said. "Not enough to understand it."

Yet.

Somewhere within the estate's network, external probes touched the perimeter—light, exploratory, testing boundaries without committing. The system registered them, adjusted, and held steady.

Mark watched him carefully.

"How much do they know?"

Thomas's gaze returned to the koi.

"They know there's a pattern," he said. "They don't know what sustains it."

He set the glass down. The sound was precise.

"Tighten up. Relocate assets. Review exposure."

Already begun.

Actions were underway.

Mark examined him.

"You're changing how this plays out."

Thomas's attention drifted briefly toward the east wing, toward Derek's suite, then came back.

"It was always changing. Pretending otherwise made it dangerous."

Mark exhaled slowly.

"Pressure isn't always the answer."

Thomas adjusted his cuff, already disengaging.

"Pressure tests what holds. Structure determines which breaks."

He turned towards the exit.

"Keep the house stable while I'm out."

Behind him, the system responded before the words finished.

"Transport prepared," Artemis said.

Thomas paused, not to rethink, but to make things right.

"Get me the Bureau agent's file. Everything. I need to know them first."

The house shifted again. Lighting recalibrated. Access layers opened. Movement aligned.

For a moment, Thomas stood still. He wasn't watching the system or the city. He was watching the pattern.

He built a world that allowed no dependence on chance, people, or unstable parts that needed protection. He sought only designed, dependable systems, controlled by intention.

That had been the flaw.

He had allowed the possibility of singular emergence—an element that could not be replicated and introduced variance. That would not happen again. He moved forward. The system followed. Progress required design, not discovery. And the design never hesitated.

CHAPTER TWENTY

Cracks in the Glass

Derek Klein gazed out the window of his penthouse, but he wasn't really seeing the city.

The Long Beach shoreline stretched below. Drones traced arcs. Synths cleaned the streets. Commuter pods threaded light between towers, a living network.

It should have steadied him. Order meant control. Control meant safety. This morning, the order felt indifferent. It would continue without him. It had already adjusted.

His reflection hovered faintly in the glass. He looked pale, his eyes rimmed red, and his jaw locked tight enough to ache. He looked like someone who hadn't slept.

He hadn't.

Every time he closed his eyes, the same moment came back. Not the whole night—just fragments. Brandon's laugh, unforced, easy, bright. Derek had always worked to earn that brightness.

Then Marcus. Neither stepping forward nor asserting. Just shifting. Small reposition. Subtle reorientation of space. Unspoken protection.

Brandon hadn't reacted. Hadn't even noticed. He had simply continued talking. Safe. Held.

Derek's breath caught, sharp and shallow. He pressed his palm to the glass, seeking something solid. I was never that for him. Not once.

He had been the edge, the tension. The friction Brandon sought to feel sharper. Derek convinced himself that meant more.

Marcus didn't need to create space. He existed in it. Brandon stepped there without pause. The realization cut clean.

Derek dragged in a breath that didn't quite settle.

"Fuck," he whispered.

The word felt thin. Useless.

Because beneath the anger, beneath the jealousy, the humiliation, the quiet recognition of being replaced, something else held.

He still loved him fiercely. Enough that watching Brandon choose someone else felt like being erased. Enough that some part of him still ached for Brandon's safety, even if it wasn't with him.

He stayed at the glass longer than he should have. Watching his own reflection.

"You knew," he said quietly. Not a question. A recognition.

Brandon's body is still beneath his hand. That almost invisible shift. He had felt it. Every time. Pressure doesn't bring him closer. It makes him disappear.

His hand lifted. Hovering. As if he could go back. Return to that moment. Choose differently. For one second, he had. He let go. Left space. Gave him a choice.

Derek's jaw locked. It hurt. It hadn't been enough. Brandon had still pulled away. Still chosen distance. Still, not been chosen.

"If I let him go…" Derek said. The words felt fragile. "I lose him."

Silence held.

"If I hold on—" He stopped. That didn't resolve either. His hand pressed to the glass. Cold and unmoving.

"I don't know how to do this without losing him." No plan. No control. Just an inability.

His breath came unevenly. The room stayed still. Nothing adjusted except something inside him, narrowing.

"If I don't act," he said slowly, "Marcus keeps him."

The name cut deep. Much deeper. Now.

"And if Marcus keeps him…" He didn't finish it. He didn't need to.

Derek turned away from the glass.

The bedroom still held him. Not memory. Presence.

The hoodie lay where Brandon left it—draped over the chair, sleeves twisted, like it had been pulled off without thought. Derek crossed the room before he realized. He picked it up. The fabric was soft, cuffs worn, faint citrus, and something quieter beneath. Familiar. He held it.

The city disappeared. So did the tension. The decision. Everything narrowed to this. He pressed the fabric briefly to his face. Closed his eyes. This is what I'm about to lose. The thought came clean. Undeniable.

He lowered it slowly. Didn't fold it. Didn't put it back. Just let it fall across his hand—then set it down.

He walked out. No more standing here. No more replaying. Stay, and he would fracture. He moved before he could reconsider.

The private link opened immediately.

One decision.

It was clean.

Irreversible.

He knew what Thomas Klein did to people like Brandon.

Not in detail. But enough.

The screen resolved.

Thomas Klein stood in his koi pavilion, serene, composed, framed by water and movement that never disrupted itself.

"Morning, Derek," Thomas said. "To what do I owe the pleasure?"

Derek's throat tightened. For a second, he almost closed the connection.

Almost stopped.

Brandon's laugh surfaced again. Marcus's hand on his back. The space Derek never held.

"I want to talk about Brandon Adams."

Thomas's expression shifted—subtle, interested.

"Ah. Yes. A promising young man."

"Don't say it." The thought came too late.

"I want him gone."

Silence followed.

Not shocked. No surprise. Just stillness.

The koi moved beneath Thomas's feet.

Uninterrupted.

"And why," Thomas asked, voice cooling slightly, "would you bring this to me?"

Derek swallowed. This was the line. Once crossed, no return. You don't mean this. He forced it down.

"I know what you're building," Derek said. "You're trying to create something that can hold emotion. Not simulate it. Sustain it."

Thomas didn't interrupt.

"And you need someone who can survive that," Derek continued. "Someone who doesn't collapse under resonance."

His pulse hammered.

"I've felt it," he said. "Brandon isn't like anyone else. He holds it."

"Go on," Thomas said.

Derek leaned forward.

"If you take him, you get what you've been trying to build," he said. "He's already forming stable connections."

"With Marcus Grant."

"Grant," Thomas said mildly. "My counsel."

"My replacement," Derek snapped. Then, quieter, bitterer, "your golden boy."

Thomas's gaze sharpened—not at the insult, but at the truth beneath it. "Marcus is not a disappointment," he said evenly. "But he is… complicated."

"If you wait," Derek added, "you lose him."

Thomas watched him. Carefully. "You're proposing we extract someone you care about," Thomas said, "and convert him into an asset."

The word care landed harder than anything else.

Derek's chest tightened. Memories collided, Brandon at the balcony. Brandon laughing. Brandon looking at him like he mattered. Then, Brandon leaning into Marcus. Choosing him. The ache sharpened.

"I'm offering you what you need," Derek said, voice steady now. "Before someone else takes it."

Thomas remained quiet.

"Subjects like Brandon do not appear twice," he said.

Derek's stomach dropped.

"There have been others," Thomas continued. "They fail. Systems fail. Minds fracture."

Derek hadn't known that. Doubt surfaced. What if—he crushed it. If he let himself see Brandon breaking, he couldn't do this. And he needed to. Didn't he?

Thomas lifted his glass.

"You're not giving me a man," he said.

"You're giving me a resource."

The word landed like judgment.

"Consider it done."

The screen went dark. No ceremony. No hesitation.

Derek stared at his reflection. For a moment, there was relief. A release of pressure. Something unbearable—decided.

Then—it hit. Hard. "What did I just do—"

The words fractured. He squeezed his eyes shut.

This is protection, he told himself. He'll be safer. Contained. Controlled.

Lies. All of them. The truth moved in. You didn't save him. You removed him. You couldn't stand to watch him choose someone else.

Derek's breath turned shallow. Uneven.

"I didn't—" No one answered. No one to argue. No forgiveness. He had traded Brandon's freedom for silence.

* * *

That afternoon, he stared at the message field. Fingers hovered.

Then, he messaged Brandon.

Hey. Can we talk? Uncle wants us both over on Friday night. Says it's important.

He sent it before he could stop. Before he could think. The reply came fast.

Sure. Send me the time.

Of course it did. Brandon said yes, trusting. Still open. Still reaching.

Derek's throat tightened. He could still stop this. Call Thomas back. Undo it. Warn him. Run.

Instead, he locked the screen. Turned away. And chose not to.

That evening, Brandon laughed at something Marcus said. Soft. Unthinking. He leaned into him without hesitation. Marcus's hand found his back. Effortless. Right.

Miles away, Derek sat in a quiet room. He told himself this was necessary—control—what moving on looked like.

His chest didn't agree. And somewhere beneath it—something had already started to break.

CHAPTER TWENTY-ONE

Breaking Point

It took days for him to realize this wasn't disappearing. Brandon was here to stay, and that was okay.

Marcus's condo had adjusted to their rhythms. As evening came, the lights softened, the ambient sound lowered, and the temperature grew milder. Outside, traffic thinned into a distant, steady wash. Inside, everything was contained.

Brandon lay beside Marcus, curled in close, his head snuggled beneath Marcus's chin. Marcus's heartbeat was steady, his thumb tracing slow, absent circles along Brandon's arm.

The Loop rested between them. Warm. Present. Quiet. Just there.

Brandon exhaled slowly, letting the day slip away.

Marcus shifted slightly. The movement was smooth.

Brandon noticed. It didn't feel wrong. Just precise in a way that didn't match the moment.

"Do you ever feel like something's coming, like a change you can't yet name?" Brandon asked softly.

Marcus's thumb paused. "Coming?" he echoed, seeking clarity.

"A shift," Brandon explained. "You just sense it—something under everything about to move, but you can't say what."

Marcus's breathing stayed even. "We face things as they come," he said quietly. "Together." He leaned down and kissed the top of Brandon's head. Gentle. Intentional.

A flicker passed through the space between them. Not sharply. Just enough. A change in the air before a storm.

Then, suddenly, fear. Not his. Marcus's.

Brandon's eyes opened. "Marcus?"

Marcus's hand resumed its motion, the same steady rhythm as before. "Babe, I'm here," he said.

Brandon didn't press. Didn't question it. But something in the Loop hummed off-key, unsettled. The warmth stayed muted. Held back. He shifted slightly, lifting himself up.

Marcus watched him. Didn't close the space. Didn't pull him back.

The distance between them wasn't avoidance. It was deliberate. The room felt still. Like the moment before something breaks.

"You're keeping something from me," Brandon said.

Marcus's breathing deepened. He could already feel it coming, where this would go, how it would break, what Brandon would need to hear to stay. He knew how to shape that.

"Yes."

Brandon waited. Marcus leaned forward, forearms resting on his knees, hands open. Grounded.

"I need to tell you something before this moves any further," he said.

Brandon stayed very still.

"Before law," Marcus continued, "I was a Field Specialist. I was trained to intervene before people understood the risk they were in. Anticipate. Adjust. Redirect."

Brandon absorbed it. "What does that mean?" he asked.

"It means I step in early," Marcus said. "Before it gets worse. Before anyone sees it."

"Redirect," Brandon repeated.

"Yes."

The Loop stirred again. Uneasy. Not warning.

Question. "The pier," Brandon said quietly. "The gull."

Marcus didn't hesitate. "Yes."

The answer came immediately. "I didn't think," Marcus said. "I moved."

"Does that make it better," Brandon asked, "or worse?"

Marcus's mouth shifted slightly. "That's the problem," he said. "I don't always know."

The silence pressed in.

"Where is the line?" Brandon asked. "How do you know when protection turns into control?"

Marcus held his gaze. "When protection becomes control," he said. "When I stop reacting and start deciding outcomes."

The words didn't echo. They settled. Brandon felt the ground shift beneath his trust. Not breaking. Separating.

"Have you ever redirected me?" he asked.

The question caught between them. Marcus didn't flinch. "No," he said. Clear. Immediate. "Not once."

Brandon held that. "But you could."

He paused.

"Yes."

That was enough. Not the capability. It was the honesty that mattered most.

"You don't trust yourself," Brandon said.

Marcus didn't look away. "No."

"And what am I?" Brandon asked quietly. "A person? Or something you manage?"

Marcus felt the answer forming, the version that would steady him, soften the edge, keep him here. He let it go. "You're the one place I refuse to run calculations," he said.

The Loop pulsed. Searching.

"That thing between us," Brandon said. "You didn't create it."

"No."

"But you understand systems."

"Yes."

"And systems can be shaped."

Marcus's jaw tightened.

Brandon didn't push further. He didn't need to. For Brandon, the connection had always felt organic. Mutual. Emergent.

For Marcus, it was also structure. And the structure could be influenced.

"Because if I ever did that to you," Marcus said quietly, "I wouldn't forgive myself."

"That's what scares me," Brandon said.

Marcus froze.

"Not that you would," Brandon added.

The truth held between them. Unsoftened.

"Why tell me now?" Brandon asked.

Marcus didn't hesitate. "Because I love you," he said.

The words landed exactly where Brandon already stood. A confirmation.

"If you stay unaware," Marcus continued, "I become something I don't want to be."

Brandon's breath caught. He had felt it. The quiet care. The restraint. The choice.

Love wasn't new. But this moment, this timing, mattered. If he answered now, it would bind him inside uncertainty. And love didn't belong there.

"And if you leave," Marcus said, softer now, "it should be with your eyes open."

Brandon stood. Not abruptly. But because he needed to move.

The connection shifted as he moved. Less like an embrace. More like focus.

Marcus stayed seated.

"If you need space," he said evenly, "I'll respect it."

Everything in him moved to close the distance. To hold. To stabilize. To decide this before it broke. He stayed where he was. The restraint stung, sharper than any argument could.

"I need to know," Brandon said quietly, "that when you touch me, it's real—not already decided by you."

Marcus took it in. Didn't argue. "I have never touched you as a strategy," he said.

Brandon believed him. That wasn't the issue.

"I should stay at my place tonight," Brandon said. Not punishment. Space.

Marcus nodded once. "I understand."

Brandon studied him. Looking for something: a crack, a tell, a shift. There was none. Only control.

"This doesn't make you a bad person," Brandon said.

"But it changes the shape of things."

"Yes."

"That doesn't mean it's over," Brandon said. "It means I need to know my choices are truly my own."

"It is," Marcus said.

"I need to feel that without questioning it," Brandon replied.

Marcus nodded. "It was never simple."

"No," Brandon said. "But it was clean."

He moved to the door. The latch clicked softly behind him. Not dramatic. Not final. Deliberate. For the first time, this wasn't something happening to him. It was something he chose. Marcus wasn't a system. He wasn't a case. He wasn't a pattern. He was a person. A risk. A reality.

And for the first time since the Loop had formed, it didn't follow. It stayed. Waiting.

Brandon stood in the quiet, the night stretching around him. He thought of the pier. Of the way Marcus had moved. Of how little he needed to do. He thought of love. And what it meant if one person could shape it. He already knew the answer. He loved him. He just didn't trust the ground beneath them yet.

CHAPTER TWENTY-TWO

The Directive

Marcus woke before dawn with the quiet certainty that something had shifted. It wasn't dangerous. Nothing that clear. This felt subtler, more like a system quietly recalibrating beneath the surface, updating without any warning.

The house was still. Brandon's side of the bed remained untouched.

Marcus lay a moment longer than needed. He registered Brandon's absence as an ache. He rose and dressed. Movements tight. Jaw clenched against the sharpness.

Composure was practiced, armor over simmering tension.

But beneath that composure, the tension, sharp and new, was unpracticed.

At the kitchen window, the city came into focus as light dawned across the horizon. Delivery drones traced clean arcs between buildings. Sanitation Synths moved in synchronized paths below.

Everything functioned exactly as designed. Every pattern was in place. Each sequence: flawless.

Yet to Marcus, it felt overly precise, almost as if the world itself was performing for someone.

Marcus checked his console. No alerts came. No anomalies appeared. Nothing at all. That, more than anything, stood out.

Brandon should have messaged by now.

Marcus stopped himself from making contact. He wanted to protect Brandon's space, believing that respecting distance would help keep him safe, even if it meant feeling helpless.

The console chimed. An invitation request. Private. Internal. Officially flagged as routine, though nothing about it felt routine at all.

Marcus opened it. Dinner. Friday. Klein Estate. Attendees: Brandon Adams, Marcus Grant. Host: Thomas Klein.

His jaw stiffened; tension spiked behind his eyes. Routine invitations didn't route through three systems or carry redundancy, but this one did. Three systems. Triple redundancy. Marcus closed the display without responding.

***

Across the city, in a different rhythm, Brandon stopped mid-step.

The Loop shifted.

It wasn't gone or truly unstable. Instead, it condensed, drawing inward, tightening. It might open again or narrow further.

He rested on the café railing, gripping cool metal. No pain. No fear. Only interference—brief, disorienting, gone before he could hold it.

The Loop had never behaved that way before; this was new.

Brandon exhaled, centering himself as the city moved. Conversations overlapped. Footsteps passed. The pattern held.

That made it worse.

He checked his console. A calendar entry pulsed. Friday. Dinner. Klein Estate. Marcus Grant is attending.

Brandon frowned, anxiety tightening his breath. Marcus hadn't said anything.

The Loop shifted again, this time uneasily. Not warning. Awareness.

Someone was looking. The sensation didn't leave. It shifted deeper instead, leaving him exposed in a way he couldn't explain.

* * *

By the time Marcus arrived at the café, Brandon had already decided not to bring up the invitation, wanting to protect them both from what it might mean. They sat facing each other in a quiet café with glass walls and clean lines, nothing to hold onto.

Marcus examined him too carefully, gaze flicking to Brandon's hands, his face, trying to read the tremor he felt beneath the stillness.

He recognized the scrutiny immediately—and didn't like it.

"You're exposed," Marcus said flatly.

Brandon blinked. "That's not how people usually start conversations."

Marcus didn't soften it. "Notice anything off today?"

Brandon hesitated. "The Loop flickered."

Marcus's breath slowed.

"Did it feel like fear?"

"No," Brandon said. "Like interference."

That was enough.

"Has anyone reached out?" Marcus asked. "Invitations. Meetings."

Brandon's mouth tightened. "Derek mentioned Friday dinner. His uncle wants us there."

Marcus didn't hide the reaction this time. "That's not a coincidence."

The Loop throbbed between them. It wasn't an alarm, but alignment.

"What aren't you telling me?" Brandon asked sharply.

Marcus held his gaze, letting the truth approach slowly.

"You're visible," he said. "Not just to people. To systems that look for patterns they don't understand."

Brandon absorbed that. "You think I'm a target."

"I think you're something they can't model," Marcus said. "And someone has decided that matters."

The Loop tightened, sharp awareness running through Brandon's chest.

"What do we do?"

Marcus didn't answer immediately. "For now, we reduce exposure."

Brandon's expression sharpened. "How?"

"Distance," Marcus said. "Less shared signal. Less predictability."

Brandon stood. "So you're pushing me away."

Marcus didn't move. "I'm trying to keep you safe."

Brandon held his gaze. Then something colder settled into place, a chill crawling down his spine and freezing the space between them.

"Friday," Brandon said. "You're going."

"Yes."

"And you don't want me to."

Marcus didn't answer.

That was answer enough. Brandon stepped back, deciding to protect himself if Marcus wouldn't let him in. Just one step. Marcus didn't follow, believing distance was the safest choice, even if it cost them connection.

"If you go, this becomes real."

"I know."

The words didn't soften anything.

Resolution settled inside him, solid, cold, not reactive or emotional. Just iron certainty in his chest.

"I decide for myself. You don't get to protect me from that."

"I'll see you tonight at my place."

Marcus took it in. No argument. No attempt to redirect.

As Brandon turned and walked away, the Loop stretched between them, thin, tight, and unresolved. It didn't break. It adapted.

* * *

Marcus remained where he was.

Still.

Because this time, he understood the cost of moving too soon.

Across the city, systems had already begun to align. And somewhere behind glass, silence, and careful design, the window for what came next was already narrowing.

CHAPTER TWENTY-THREE

The Last Quiet

The sky outside Brandon's bedroom window deepened to indigo as night settled in. City lights softened through the marine layer, softening Seal Beach into a glow as well as shadow. Inside the house, everything stilled. No music. No projections. Only the slight trace of ocean air slid through the open rooftop door.

The quiet felt intentional.

As if the world itself is holding its breath.

Marcus lay on his side, stroking the skin on Brandon's bare chest. Their skin still carried heat from the rooftop spa, from the shower, from everything they had allowed themselves to feel. But something heavier had remained between them.

Truth.

Brandon leaned into the touch and exhaled. "Sometimes I think… If I close my eyes long enough, I can freeze a moment like this. Just hold it."

Marcus's mouth curved, though tension remained behind his eyes. "I feel that too. Like we're standing on the edge of something fragile."

Brandon turned until their faces hovered inches apart. "Maybe it doesn't have to last forever. Maybe it just has to be real."

Their mouths touched. Loving. A slow folding inward.

Brandon slid closer, thigh pressing between Marcus's legs. Heat built where their bodies met, hard and insistent. Marcus's hand slid up Brandon's neck, fingers threading into his hair as the kiss deepened. Tongues met, tasting salt and want. Marcus dragged his mouth along Brandon's jaw, then lower, sucking at the skin beneath his ear until Brandon's breath fractured.

Marcus shifted downward. He licked across Brandon's nipple, then took it between his teeth, tugging just enough to pull a sharp inhale from him. His hand wrapped around Brandon's cock, stroking with steady pressure while his mouth worked the other nipple. Brandon arched, hips lifting off the bed, a low sound escaping his throat.

"I need to taste you," Marcus said, voice husky. He moved lower, pressing kisses down Brandon's stomach. When he reached Brandon's cock, he licked a slow stripe from base to tip, then took the head into his mouth. Heat and suction wrapped him. Marcus took him farther, tongue pressing along the underside, one hand stroking what his mouth couldn't reach. Brandon's fingers tightened in Marcus's hair, not guiding, just holding on as pleasure spiked through him.

Marcus kept control, setting the rhythm, sucking with focused intent while his free hand cupped Brandon's balls. The Loop sparked—brief, bright—letting Brandon feel Marcus's own heavy arousal, the satisfaction of drawing those broken sounds from the man he loved. Brandon's thighs trembled. His hips rocked once before he caught himself.

Marcus pulled off with a wet sound, kissed the inside of Brandon's thigh, then took him in again, deeper this time. He worked him thoroughly until Brandon's breath came in uneven pulls and his grip tightened.

Then Marcus crawled back up. Their mouths crashed together, sharing the taste of Brandon on Marcus's tongue. Brandon rolled them, kissing down Marcus's chest, but his movements carried urgency born of emotion rather than precision. He licked across Marcus's nipple, then lower, taking Marcus's cock into his mouth with open hunger. He sucked hard, cheeks hollowing, one hand stroking in tight pulls while the other gripped Marcus's hip.

Marcus watched him, chest rising fast. The Loop sparked again, sharper this time, letting him feel the raw need behind Brandon's actions, the way giving pleasure grounded him after everything they had survived.

They stayed like that, mouths and hands moving, until both were aching, skin damp with sweat. Marcus finally reached for the lube. He coated himself, then guided Brandon's hand to help slick him further, their fingers sliding together over heated skin.

Brandon straddled him. He took Marcus inside inch by inch, the stretch pulling a rough sound from his throat. For one long moment, they held completely still, foreheads pressed together, breath intermingling. Nothing moved except the slight quiver in Brandon's thighs and the mutual pounding of their hearts.

Then the Loop ignited, bright, sudden, flooding them with memory.

Marcus saw it all at once:

The boy is alone in his bedroom, sketching connections no one else could see.

The ache of being unseen.

The hollow quiet after almost-love.

The desperate need to be chosen. Kept.

And Marcus sensed his own instincts rise in sharp contrast, the discipline of never asking for too much, the habit of leaving first, the reflex to withdraw before he could be left behind. The contrast struck as a fracture. He broke open under it, something fierce and protective answering Brandon's vulnerability.

Brandon moved, hips rolling with raw emotion. This wasn't careful choreography. It was resolved, made flesh. Marcus was not something to experience. He was something to guard.

Brandon leaned down, forehead against Marcus's. "It's not just sex. You're in me."

Emotion surged fast enough to crack Marcus open. The plan flickered at the edge of his mind—Friday, the danger, the machinery already in motion. Fear clamped down.

He kissed Brandon instead. Deep. Certain.

It started as pressure.

Weight.

Breath.

Brandon rolled his hips in tight circles, dragging Marcus through him. Marcus answered with deeper thrusts, hands gripping Brandon's back, fingers digging in. Every shift echoed between them through the Loop. Heat built. Friction. The wet slide of bodies. The room filled with the scent of sweat and arousal and them.

They edged closer. Control frayed.

When the crest rose, they didn't slow. They pushed through it.

Short breaths. Locked muscles. Brandon clenched hard around him as release tore through his body, spilling hot between them. Marcus followed right behind, buried deep, pulsing in steady waves that dragged them both under. The Loop flared once more, intense, blinding, then faded into warmth.

For a suspended moment, everything stopped.

No guilt.

No distance.

Just the heavy press of bodies and the quiet truth that the cost had already begun.

Afterward, they stayed tangled. Breathing slowing. Skin cooling against damp sheets. The Loop settled into something quieter. More intimate. More dangerous.

Brandon's cheek rested on Marcus's chest. Marcus traced patterns along his spine.

Neither spoke.

Neither moved.

The silence held everything they weren't saying:

This feels right.

This will cost us everything.

Neither of us wants to stop.

They stayed like that until sleep found them.

* * *

Brandon woke first. He didn't move. Just watched the ceiling.

Memory drifted in fragments, not Marcus's. His own. Moments where he had stepped in without thinking. Taken on weight that wasn't his. He had always been good at standing watch. He just hadn't known what he was waiting for.

Marcus shifted beside him. "Brandon… no matter what happens, I want you to know—I love you."

Brandon turned, pressing a finger gently to his lips. "I love you too. Just stay with me. Here."

Marcus nodded.

He didn't trust himself to say more.

* * *

Outside, the marine layer thickened. Fog rolled in from the ocean.

A gull drifted past the window. Marcus's eyes tracked its path, trajectory too clean, wingbeats too evenly spaced, like something programmed rather than alive. Its shadow slid across the glass.

Brandon didn't see it.

Marcus did.

And for the first time that night, he chose to look away from Brandon. Not toward the threat, but away from the man whose trust he was already breaking.

* * *

Across the city—

Derek sat in a house that no longer felt like his.

Thomas finalized the extraction plan.

Bureau signals moved quietly through backchannels.

Acquisition teams are aligned.

* * *

Inside the room, two men lay curled together.

Hearts synced.

Bodies still carrying the truth of what they had chosen.

Time, held gently between them, was already breaking.

CHAPTER TWENTY-FOUR

The Fall

The sun touched the horizon as the car sped to Thomas Klein's estate. Fog hung low, bringing salt and cold inland. A few stars penetrated the marine layer, dim yet persistent.

Brandon looked out the windshield, thinking of Marcus and the stillness. The night before, something had settled inside him. It wasn't a revelation, just a sense of acceptance.

He wasn't drifting anymore.

The vehicle slowed at the gate. A scan swept the glass, checking biometrics, neural cadence, and vehicle ID. It lasted just long enough to do its job, then stopped.

A chime. Access granted.

The gate parted with a hydraulic whisper.

Brandon exhaled and smoothed his Henley. He wore dark jeans and no jacket, aiming for casual but intentional.

Marcus's voice echoed in his mind, steady but reluctant. "I can still join you, Brandon, but I will respect your wishes."

Brandon shook his head. "If Marcus comes, it turns into a confrontation. If I go alone, it stays personal."

A knot formed in his chest as he spoke. Certainty slipped; his voice turned brittle, and conviction felt borrowed.

The car eased to a stop beneath the arched entryway. Brandon stepped out, shoulders rising and falling as he drew a steadying breath.

Anxiety pricked under his skin, a raw current. His palms grew damp, and his breathing faltered; something beneath the surface seemed unsteady.

Not enough to turn back.

Enough to notice.

Derek greeted him at the door, gripping a glass of Malbec. His smile forced, eyes shining bright, knuckles pale.

"Brandon. Thanks for coming."

"Of course."

Derek's smile stayed, practiced but never landing.

Brandon accepted the wine and walked in.

The house smelt of sandalwood and engineered calm, a luxury designed to lower defenses. Synths moved through, adjusting light and mood to emotional presets.

It felt like walking into a mood.

"Your uncle around?" Brandon asked lightly.

"Upstairs. He wanted us to catch up first."

They entered the rear lounge. Sconces cast a warm light over the pool beyond the glass. Water glistened, still and perfect.

It should have felt serene, but quiet tension built up beneath the surface. Brandon sensed the mood had shifted.

Instead, Brandon's nerves tingled. A low alert hummed under his skin, and he felt as if hidden eyes were watching him.

Derek motioned toward a chaise. "Sit?"

Brandon sat, resting the wine in his lap.

"You seem… different," Derek said after a moment. "Calmer. Happier."

Brandon smiled without thinking. "I am."

"With Marcus."

"Yes."

Mentioning Marcus increased the tension, leaving their mutual past dense in the silence.

A muscle jumped in Derek's jaw. "I still remember what we had."

Brandon held his gaze. "So do I. But I wasn't in love. You read my note. We had an agreement. We are friends. I want that to continue, but I am not in love with you, Derek."

Derek looked away, his breath unsteady. "It was love for me."

A tense silence followed, each second sharp with hurt and things unsaid.

Then Thomas's voice came through the open patio doors, smooth and calm.

"Gentlemen. Join me. Dinner is served."

* * *

The dining room was carefully elegant. Crystal decanters glowed amber, wines rested in custom holders, and Synth stewards moved softly through the space.

Thomas rose as they entered.

"Brandon. Good to see you again. We barely scratched the surface of our most recent conversation before my guests carried me away."

Brandon blinked. He hadn't realized Thomas meant it so seriously.

"I notice people who observe," Thomas continued. "You had the posture of a photographer, even without your camera."

Brandon smiled politely, though a chill slid along his spine. "I try to see what's real."

Thomas's eyes flickered with interest. "Exactly why we wanted you here. Holotec is launching a new adaptive nanotech line. Derek will oversee creative direction. We'd like you behind the lens."

Derek brightened instantly. "This could be huge, Bran. Something meaningful. Together."

"You shoot. I style. We collaborate," Derek said quickly. "Like we always talked about."

Thomas observed with quiet amusement.

Brandon lifted his glass.

For a moment, neither drank. The room waited.

Crystal touched crystal.

Marcus.

Distant. Uneasy.

Fear scratched at Brandon's chest as cold fingers tightened around his heart.

Brandon inhaled too fast.

"Everything okay?" Derek asked.

"Yeah," Brandon said, steadying himself.

Thomas's gaze focused.

He looked not with concern, but with precise, calculating interest. He was reassessing Brandon with new intent.

After dinner, Thomas rose. "Derek has something upstairs he'd like to show you. A preview."

Derek nodded eagerly. "Let's head up to my suite."

Brandon followed, feeling more uneasy.

In Derek's suite, a small glass bottle rested on a sleek side table, emitting a soft glow. Inside, a luminous mist stuck to the glass, shining like starlight.

"It's a skin hydrator," Derek said. "Adaptive nanotech. First prototype."

Brandon turned it, watching light refract. "And you want me to test it."

Derek swallowed. "Uncle said it would mean more coming from you."

Brandon hesitated.

A sudden, cold rush of dread ran through him.

And then it happened.

Marcus's hand at his sternum.

Stay.

The word was not dramatic.

It was steady.

Brandon inhaled once, anchoring himself.

Then he nodded.

He lifted the bottle and misted his face.

Cool droplets touched his skin.

The world swayed.

The wineglass fell from his hand and shattered.

"Derek…" Brandon whispered, panic rising through his voice as his knees gave out.

The floor came toward him in slow motion.

His body slipped out of his control, panic scraping his mind in sharp bursts as helplessness seized him.

Hands caught him.

Not just Derek's hands.

***

Straps closed over his wrists.

Containment force bands locked against his temples and sternum.

A flow of gold energy responded automatically.

The projection ring overhead burst with filaments of light, bright and alive.

Behind smart glass near Thomas's office, a private lab surged to life.

Brandon lay restrained on a contoured platform, naked under sterile lights. Synths moved with precise coordination as scanning arms passed over his body, measuring bioelectric flux, endocrine response, and neural resonance.

Thomas observed from behind safety glass, Macallan in hand.

A technician glanced at the monitors. "Hallucinogen stable. Subject entering erotic-recall simulation. All input interpreted as partner contact."

On the platform, Brandon's body arched, his breath catching, and his fingers curling into imagined sheets. The nanotech created an illusion: warm hands, not cold straps, traced his collarbone and moved down his chest, thumbs circling his nipples until they hardened. A mouth followed, bringing familiar pressure—Marcus's tongue teasing, tasting salt and want. Brandon gasped, his hips lifting on instinct.

The Loop flickered then fractured, echoing the phantom touch back twice, then three times. Every touch landed both on his skin and deeper, in the place where pleasure met fear.

Phantom fingers slid lower, parting thighs with deliberate slowness. A tongue circled the head of his arousal—slow, wet heat—then took him deeper, suction pulling a low, broken moan from his throat. Brandon's back bowed, wrists straining against restraints he no longer fully felt.

The illusion deepened. A body pressed over him—Marcus's weight, heat, scent—cock sliding against his, slick and insistent. Then pressure at his entrance—slow push, stretch, fill. Brandon's breath shattered into whimpers; his hips rocked up to meet each thrust, body clenching around the phantom intrusion as if it were real.

Through the breaking Loop, faint echoes of Marcus reached him—first worry, then alarm—but they faded into the simulation's loop. Pleasure kept building: slow movements turning urgent, a hand stroking him in rhythm, thumb pressing the sensitive underside until his vision blurred gold.

He tried to resist, knowing it wasn't Marcus and not his choice, but his body betrayed him, quivering on the edge. The illusion kept him there, holding him back, slowing just as climax neared, then surging again, until he broke.

Release tore through him, violent and consuming. His muscles seized, a choked cry escaped, and waves pulsed outward, gold flaring across the monitors. The simulation didn't stop; it kept going, drawing another peak, then a third, until Brandon's body shook with overstimulation and tears fell from his closed eyes.

Not due to pain.

Shame and betrayal thundered through him, knocking the air from his lungs. Pleasure had become a violation, and intimacy, once cherished, became a sharp weapon. A lonely, unbreakable line was drawn inside him.

Monitors spiked—gold arcs flaring violently.

"Resonance spike confirmed."

"Amplitude exceeding predicted baseline."

"Output extraordinary. Bleed confirmed."

A technician leaned closer. "Match confirmed. Previous scan picked this up. Matches an anomaly already in the archive."

No one reacted.

It scrolled like routine.

"Dormant classification validated."

The system pulsed in acknowledgment.

"Scanner confirmation complete."

"Prepare transport," Thomas ordered.

Derek's lips parted, horror freezing his words before sound escaped.

Straps detached; re-secured to a mobile gurney.

Brandon tried to force the Loop outward—not to gain power.

For connection.

He reached for Marcus.

For hesitation.

For steadiness.

He found nothing but distance.

The sedation deepened.

The last thing he felt was an aching, iron emptiness.

Not Derek.

Not Marcus.

Just the awareness that something had seen him long before tonight.

And it had never lost sight of him. Years of quiet observation had brought this moment about.

Darkness enveloped him.

* * *

Miles away, Marcus sat at Brandon's dining table amid scattered briefs and encrypted files.

He rubbed his eyes.

The Loop snapped.

Not faded.

Snapped.

A violent jolt slammed into his chest.

For half a breath, he felt Brandon—close, terrified, reaching.

Brandon.

Fear.

Disorientation.

Marcus felt it before he understood it.

Absence.

The Loop didn't weaken—it collapsed, as if something that had always been there had been removed all at once, leaving nothing for his body to orient around.

For a moment, he didn't move.

Because there was nowhere to go.

His chest tightened—not sharp, not panicked—just… wrong. Like breathing had lost its reference point. Like his body had forgotten what it was stabilizing for.

"Brandon," he said.

The name didn't land anywhere.

That was the first fracture.

He reached for the connection carefully, the way he always did, never forcing it.

Nothing answered.

No echo.

No resistance.

No distortion.

Just clean, empty silence.

His hand pressed flat against his sternum, as if he could hold the space closed.

He couldn't.

The realization didn't arrive in panic.

It arrived as certainty.

Whatever had been there—

whatever had anchored him—

was gone.

His knees bent slightly, not enough to fall, just enough that his body stopped trusting itself to remain upright.

He tried again.

"Stay."

The word broke apart before it left his mouth.

There was nothing to hold onto.

And for the first time in years, not in systems, not in law, not in anything,

Marcus had no next move.

The surge burned through until nothing was left to burn.

What remained was exhaustion, deep and absolute.

He did not fall asleep.

He shut down.

CHAPTER TWENTY-FIVE

After the Glass

The suite still carried a faint citrus scent. Derek hadn't noticed it when Brandon collapsed. The glass broke. The system chimed. Now, it was the only thing remaining. The wineglass lay shattered on the marble. A thin ribbon of red crept toward the grout line. It stopped—like something that had tried to move but failed. The air hung in suspension. Not quiet—waiting.

Derek stood where he caught him, frozen not by indecision, but because moving would crystallize fear. Helplessness flickered beneath his stillness. His hands trembled. He pressed them together to stop it. It didn't work.

He entered the hallway. The transition felt off—unnaturally smooth. The corridor stretched ahead, with sharp lines. Muted lighting pressed into a quiet stillness. Doors hissed open and shut deliberately. Elevators descended smoothly. The house recalibrated itself with mechanical precision. Everything kept moving, as if nothing had happened.

Derek walked, numbness settling in as grief pressed closer, each step marking the slow encroachment of normalcy into shock. Each step landed without weight, as if the ground wasn't fully there. The further he moved from the suite, the heavier the normalcy pressed in. That was worse. Because it meant something else entirely. This had been absorbed already.

The monitoring chamber lights were dim. The projection ring hung overhead, unused. The platform stood there, empty. Derek stopped—not at the door, but a few steps back, as if distance might change what he was seeing. It didn't. The emptiness was stark. Complete. Nothing more to understand.

A technician passed him. Didn't look at him.

"Transport complete."

Derek's voice caught in his throat, stuck.

"Where?"

"Mojave."

The word didn't land. Then, it did.

"The Mojave phase lab is optimized for this class of subject."

Subject. Derek flinched, but not for Brandon—he did it for himself. In that moment, shame pierced his guilt, turning it inward. He realized this, transforming his guilt into self-inflicted pain. He moved toward the glass, slower now, as if he was approaching something that could break further if he got too close. His hand pressed firmly against it. Cold, unyielding, unforgiving.

"I didn't know," he said. The words fell apart the moment they left him. Because something inside him answered immediately: You did. Not the details. Not the outcome. But the direction. He had chosen this path. The memory hit. Brandon's body was arching. The gold arcs flared beneath suppression bands. The voice spoke, "Output extraordinary." Not concerned or hesitant, a measurement. Derek's stomach turned. Not gradually. All at once.

He leaned forward. A sharp, dry retch. Nothing came up. His body tried again. Still nothing. There was nothing left to give. He stayed bent over the console longer than he should have. Breathing—or trying to breathe. Air moved in without settling. His chest tightened, as if his body no longer trusted what it was meant to stabilize. This wasn't containment. This wasn't control. This wasn't a correction. This was consumption.

His grip locked, knuckles whitening on the console's edge. Because if he let go, he might fall.

"I thought—" He stopped. No version of that sentence could survive the test of reality. Not: I thought he'd be safe. I thought it would scare him. I thought Thomas would do something. None of it held. He had taken a person and handed him over to a system.

"Derek." Mark's voice didn't echo.

Derek didn't turn. "I loved him." The words broke out of him—not controlled, not measured. Too late.

Mark stepped closer. "You tried to own him." No anger. No judgment. Just truth.

He shook his head feebly. The movement was unconvincing. Because now he could see it—clearly, plainly, without defense. This wasn't love. This was control disguised as love. "I didn't think he would disappear," Derek said. And that was the last lie. The final one that truly mattered. The hollow inside him shifted from defensive lies to the ache of truth.

Mark didn't answer immediately because the truth didn't need reinforcement.

"He's stable enough for transport." Derek's knees bent slightly, not enough to fall. Doubt crept in, unseating the last of his confidence. His body betrayed unsettled emotion, trembling with uncertainty. He readjusted, a subtle correction, as if relearning balance in a room that was constant. "I thought he would choose me." The words came out quieter now—smaller, stripped.

Mark didn't interrupt. Didn't soften it.

Derek stared at the empty platform. This was protection and was understood with absolute clarity—Brandon hadn't chosen Marcus. Brandon had chosen himself. And Derek had taken away that choice. The distinction sank in. Guilt settled, becoming a steady ache rather than a sharp shock. Irreversible.

"I delivered him," Derek said. Not to Mark. Not to the room. To himself. And there was nothing left to argue with. Silence followed. Not empty. Settled. Like something had reached its conclusion.

Mark's hand came to rest on his shoulder. "You need to leave."

Derek blinked. "What?"

"Not because you're guilty," Mark said. "Because you're visible. You're attached to him. To Thomas. That makes you leverage."

"I don't care about leverage," Derek snapped.

"I know."

Derek looked back at the glass. The platform. The absence. "I thought he would choose me." The words felt thinner now, fading into resignation as the last hope for vindication quietly dissolved. "I thought if I pushed harder… if I proved it…"

He stopped. Because now he understood—He hadn't proven anything. He had taken.

Mark's hand tightened slightly. "Thomas crossed a line."

Derek looked at him. "You're saying that?"

"Yes." No hesitation.

"And you're staying?" Derek asked.

Mark didn't answer. Instead, he said, "I can protect you." He paused. "Travel Accounts, Distance." Exile not named but clear.

Derek nodded slowly. He deserved to be removed. He had been reckless. And reckless men caused collateral damage. He took one last look at the platform. "This time," he said quietly, "nothing snapped."

He paused.

"It settled." Behind them, the estate lighting recalibrated. Doors opened. Closed. The system kept running. And far beneath the desert, Brandon Adams disappeared into something Derek no longer understood. It wasn't jealousy that hollowed him out; it was devastation. And the terrible clarity that he had not lost Brandon to Marcus. The real devastation now was clear—he had delivered him to something that did not care who he loved. The emotional devastation completely overshadowed jealousy.

CHAPTER TWENTY-SIX

Echoes

Marcus woke alone.

He didn't wake with a start. There was no jolt or gasp. Instead, a slow awareness crept in, telling him that something important had changed.

His body felt off, his mind caught up. He was heavy and drained, like every part of him had shut down without warning.

The space beside him was still warm, the sheets holding the faint shape of Brandon's body. Brandon's scent—lavender, cedar, sun-warmed skin—hung in the air like a memory that didn't know it was gone, familiar enough to hurt.

The smartglass lightened from night-blue to pale dawn.

He refused to look at it.

The ache in his chest slowly surfaced. First came surprise, then a deep, hollow pain he couldn't ignore.

The Loop was gone.

He sat up quickly, breath catching as the sense of absence grew. The connection wasn't just quiet or distant.

But now it was simply missing.

It had been torn away, leaving his nerves tingling as if his skin was suddenly exposed to cold air.

Memories of last night rushed back to him, not like a dream, but like a blow.

Brandon's presence was flooding the Loop.

A surge of panic.

A raw, uncontrolled reach.

Then, at the moment the Dreaming Gate collapsed inward,

Silence.

Emptiness.

Everything felt wrong.

Marcus swung his legs out of bed, his hands shaking as he pulled on his jeans. He walked into the hallway, hoping that moving would help him feel normal again.

"Artemis," he rasped. "Show me Brandon's last outbound message."

The house answered in its infuriatingly calm voice.

"No messages have been sent since 19:02 last evening."

Marcus pulled up their thread anyway.

The final entry was a heart emoji.

Brandon's.

Sent just before he'd left for Derek's.

A tight, anxious fear squeezed Marcus's chest. His breath grew shallow as panic rose with the realization.

He called.

Once.

Twice.

Three times.

No answer.

By the fourth call, panic took over. Fear wasn't just a feeling anymore—it pushed him to act.

He called Tiago.

"Hey," Tiago answered, voice thick with sleep. "What's—"

"Brandon's missing."

There was silence, then Tiago snapped fully awake.

"Missing how?" Tiago said.

"He went to Derek's last night. No calls. No messages. Artemis says his biometrics dropped off the grid twelve hours ago."

A sharp curse.

"I'm coming over."

The line went dead.

* * *

Less than an hour later, after everyone arrived, tension filled Brandon's home.

Marcus paced the living room, tense and restless. Tiago stood by the kitchen island, his eyes red and his hands flexing with worry. Sam and Teri worked at the main console, Bureau-grade systems connected to Brandon's network.

The house felt wrong without him.

It was too quiet.

And the silence was far too deep.

It felt like something vital was missing. The house was still standing, but it felt like it could fall apart at any moment.

Sam's fingers flew across the console.

"Pulling logs. Neural registry, environmental sensors, Synth navigation data."

Teri layered satellite overlays on top of the feeds.

Teri said, "Cross-referencing Horizon's movement. Acquisition units were active last night. Belmont Heights."

"We confirm the location, then we move," Teri said.

Marcus stopped pacing.

"We don't wait for confirmation. If something happened, it happened at Klein's."

Sam's screen pulsed.

She froze.

Sam stared at her screen. "Marcus… Brandon's neural imprint spiked at 20:17. Massive theta-range activity."

Tiago swallowed.

"Dream-state."

Sam shook her head, disagreement clear on her face.

Sam's voice grew tense. "No. This isn't sleep. Forced, maybe—synthetic amplification."

She stopped.

Marcus stepped closer.

"Then what?"

"Then his trace vanished."

"Then we assume extraction," Teri said.

The word hit hard.

"Vanished," Marcus repeated. "What does that mean?"

"Blocked. Masked. Rerouted," Sam said. "Take your pick."

The memory hit Marcus hard: Brandon reaching for him through the Loop, desperation clawing across their connection.

Then came the sudden, brutal break.

Tiago cleared his throat.

"Derek sent me a message."

Marcus turned slowly.

"One word."

Tiago held up his comm.

Forgive.

The room went still.

Marcus's voice dropped, shifting from anger to a quieter, sharper grief. His heart ached as he spoke, his emotions turning from accusation to pain.

"He set Brandon up."

Sam hesitated.

"We can't assume Derek knew the full scope—"

"I don't care what he knew," Marcus snapped. "He delivered him."

"Doesn't change what we do next," Teri said.

No one argued.

Sam's fingers froze over the console.

"Wait."

The room went still.

"What?" Marcus asked.

Sam expanded the neural trace Brandon had triggered before the signal vanished. The waveform looked broken at first—static, dead air where the connection should have continued.

Then she isolated the last two seconds.

"There's bleed," she said quietly.

"From what?" Teri asked.

"From the routing layer. The signal didn't disappear—it bounced."

Sam pulled up the city infrastructure grid. Abandoned industrial nodes flickered across the map like dormant nerves.

Marcus leaned closer.

"Where?"

Sam highlighted one.

A dead freight terminal along the Belmont corridor.

"That relay hasn't been active in years," Teri said.

"Exactly," Sam replied. "Which means nobody's watching it."

Marcus was already moving toward the door.

"Gear up."

* * *

At the abandoned Belmont corridor terminal, wind howled through rusted steel.

Marcus moved fast, breath shallow, heart hammering as the pull intensified.

"There," he whispered. "He's close."

The Loop flared.

But changed.

Instead, it was being shaped.

Marcus dropped to one knee, gasping as a rush of sensation hit him—heat, familiarity, and the feeling of Brandon's presence.

"I'm here," Marcus said.

And this time it wasn't automatic.

It was not born of reflex.

His voice broke on the word 'here.' His breath was rough, not steady. He paused, listening for any sign that Brandon could hear him.

"Babe, I'm here," he repeated softly.

That was how he always said it.

Relief answered him.

For a split second.

Warm.

Recognizable.

Then,

Reversal.

The resonance flipped, slamming back like feedback. Pain shot through his chest as the echo faded.

Sam shouted.

"Marcus—disconnect!"

Too late.

The signal died.

The facility went dark.

Silence returned, heavier than before, settling in Marcus's chest as shock faded into despair and numbness.

* * *

They got him out before he collapsed.

Marcus sat against cold concrete, shaking, unable to steady his hands.

"That was him," Marcus said hoarsely.

Sam swallowed. "No. It was a mirror."

"A trap," Teri said. "Built from Brandon's imprint."

"They used him," Marcus said.

"Yes," Teri replied. "And now they know how far you'll follow."

Marcus pressed his palm to his chest.

The Loop was still gone.

But the absence hurt differently now. It was sharper, the sting of hope turning right back into loss.

It was worse now.

For a moment—just a moment—he'd felt something real in the noise.

Brandon had known the difference.

And Marcus had answered the only way he knew how.

With breath.

With hesitation.

With choice.

And that, at least, could not be copied.

Marcus stayed seated on the concrete long after the echo died.

Not because he didn't know what to do.

Because he did. And this time, his certainty was sharpened by loss, determination mixing with the ache.

His first instinct: escalate, break down doors, call in favors, force truth into the open.

He let that instinct crest.

Then he let it pass.

He pushed himself to his feet slowly.

"Next time," he said quietly, more to himself than to the others, "we don't run toward the noise."

Sam watched him carefully.

"We change the terrain."

CHAPTER TWENTY-SEVEN

Inside the System

Brandon woke to light that never changed.

The light never flickered or changed with the time of day. It stayed steady, cold, and indifferent. Brandon lay still for a while—not because he was unable to move, but because he sensed something in the room was already watching him.

Sensation returned to him gradually: the cold against his back, something restraining his wrists, and a strange pressure at his temples. Then his memories flooded back—all at once—the mist, Derek, the fall. He opened his eyes, his heart pounding, every breath sharp with fear. Glass. White light. The ring above him. This wasn't just a room; it was a system. He saw movement beyond the glass. They weren't guards, but observers watching him.

Dr. Elan Voss appeared in view. She observed his breathing carefully, timing each inhale and watching his reaction. It took too long. "You're stabilizing." Her tone was not relieved, just assured.

"Where am I?" Brandon asked, his throat dry.

"Mojave." Her tone didn't soften.

"Why?"

She maintained his gaze. "As you are, you're rare."

A breath that almost became a laugh caught in his chest. "You drugged me."

"You reacted."

A Synth approached, with blue light flowing over him. The scan felt precise, almost personal, as if it was measuring and comparing everything about him. Beyond the glass, the observers adjusted their focus—an unspoken sign that something new was beginning.

"You're mapping the Loop," Brandon said quietly.

"Yes." Something moved behind her. "Marcus is gone."

Her words hit him hard. His jaw clenched, a shiver of grief barely held back. Brandon didn't respond. He stayed perfectly still.

The room watched. Now he felt it—the system's anticipation, not just the glass or the observers. It was waiting to understand him.

He inhaled. Something seized him, not in the air but inside him. A sudden warmth spread through his body, catching him off guard. It wasn't a thought or a memory—just a sensation. A hand at his waist. Marcus.

He could still feel Marcus's touch—steady and grounding, like the moment right before something happens, before any decision is made. Brandon's breath caught; a tremor shook him, the memory and loss nearly breaking him. He steadied himself, bracing inwardly against grief's pull. His body reacted immediately, his chest tightening and a pull deep inside him that had nothing to do with the room.

The system responded immediately. Data shifted.

"Spike detected."

The warmth diminished—not disappeared, but settled. Brandon exhaled slowly. He closed his eyes and lingered in the feeling just long enough to remember it before it drifted away.

"Run a simulation," Elan said.

The lights dimmed suddenly, signaling a change in the environment. A faint hum grew louder, and the air shifted, blending the present with what was projected—Brandon prepared for what was to come. Marcus appeared.

Brandon's breath caught, and for a moment, he wished it was real.

Marcus moved closer, reaching out with his hand.

It was too slick, too sure. Marcus would have hesitated. That was where it fell apart. Brandon turned his head. The Loop wavered.

"Pause simulation," Elan said.

The image faded away. Silence settled again, signaling the sudden end of the simulation and returning the room to its sterile current state.

She studied him. "Why did you stop?"

"That wasn't him."

The output stopped. She didn't interrupt it.

"Explain."

"He didn't ask."

It wasn't just a theory; it was a failure.

"Marcus always asks."

The monitors shifted, gold patterns moving as they recalibrated.

"Record that," Elan said. Then, after only a brief pause, "Run it again."

The projection ring ignited. Marcus appeared again, sharper and more precise, but still not quite right.

"You're holding something back," the simulation said.

"You're making progress," Brandon replied.

The copy stepped forward again. He felt the warmth once more. Still wrong. Brandon let it pass through him.

"You're not responding."

"I am," Brandon said quietly. "Just not the way you expect."

The projection drew nearer, persistent but unfinished.

Brandon turned inward. The pier, salt air, wind. Marcus beside him, still, waiting. The warmth shifted, growing stronger until it felt real. For a moment, someone—or something—appeared to respond to him. Marcus is distant and alive. "He's there," Brandon said. Hope and surprise seeped into his voice.

"Terminate," Elan said sharply. The connection broke suddenly and hard.

Gone.

The absence cut deep into him, raw and physical, sharper and more brutal than any simulation before. Voices rose behind the glass.

"That left containment—"

"It dropped sequence—"

"It went somewhere—"

Elan didn't look at Brandon. "You sent that somewhere." He didn't answer. He didn't need to.

They had all felt it. Which meant Marcus had, too.

Time stretched. No simulation. No immediate correction. That was new.

Then, as the tension subsided, a different energy rose. Across the chamber, a new presence awakened, drawing Brandon's attention. Another pod. Tiago. Alive. Watching.

The system had made a mistake. It had let him see. Inside, his resolve changed—deliberate and steady. When the simulation returned, Marcus was better, closer. The pause was almost right. The timing was nearly human.

Brandon let the response rise, then stopped. The system pushed, and he let it. Then he removed the ending, causing the model to stall.

"Signal degradation—"

"No—"

"It's fragmenting—"

* * *

Miles away, Marcus sensed it—not as clarity, but as an interruption. "He's doing it again."

* * *

Inside the chamber, the projection faltered. The ring dimmed. The system hesitated.

Elan leaned closer. "He's not reacting," she said. "He's making a choice."

Brandon lay still, every muscle taut, breath shaking as he wrestled fear and hope. The Loop settled deep in his chest. It didn't reach out or expand. It held. He understood now. They weren't trying to break him. That meant he still had time. And time meant he still had a choice.

CHAPTER TWENTY-EIGHT

Exposure

Tiago felt it before he understood it, not data, not alerts, but pressure. Something in the system is shifting, quietly and precisely, like a structure beginning to fail under its own weight.

Across the city, Marcus was already moving. Marcus didn't move without cause, which meant whatever this was, it was already real.

Tiago's office at Horizon BioTech was bright, active, alive with motion, and completely empty. Animated panels rippled with optimism, growth curves, synthetic empathy models, and projected futures designed to reassure, but none of it reached him.

Teri stood near the holoscreen, scrolling through layered files with deliberate precision. She wasn't searching anymore. She was confirming.

Tiago watched the system unfold.

Project trees branched into restricted layers. Ethical safeguards dissolved into administrative bypasses. Funding streams looped through shell allocations, burying oversight inside compliance language.

Clean. Elegant. Invisible.

Then, he noticed it, his authorization, his name, attached.

"No."

The word barely formed before it broke. His hand slammed against the glass table, the sharp crack cutting through the room.

This wasn't theoretical. This wasn't abstract.

This was operational. Live.

"They built it," he said, voice tightening. "They actually built it."

Teri didn't look up. "They didn't build it," she said. "You did."

The screen flickered, a secondary feed surfacing without prompt, not random, but routed.

Tiago froze.

Brandon.

Contained. Shoulders drawn inward, not broken, but compressed. His skin was pale beneath sterile light, but his gaze was focused and alert, cutting through the glass rather than reflecting it.

Looking.

Not at the room. Through it.

Tiago's breath caught. "They're using him," he said. "They're using people."

Teri stopped scrolling. "They extracted from him," she said. "They call him a stabilizing vector."

The words settled like a verdict.

"The missing link."

Tiago paced, too fast, too tight, his thoughts trying to outrun what was already clear.

"I didn't approve this," he said. "I would never—"

"But you did."

Her voice didn't rise. That made it worse.

"You scaled ethics into process," she continued. "You trusted structure over visibility."

Tiago shook his head. "You think I'd condone this? Turning people into test subjects? Building emotional prisons?"

"You didn't condone it," she said. "You enabled it."

That hit him hard. No defense left.

Tiago sank into the chair. The room hadn't changed, but something inside it had.

"What now?" he asked.

Teri finally turned. "Now you stop pretending this is containable."

"Shut it down," she said. "And make sure it can't hide."

Tiago nodded slowly as shock faded and something sharper took its place.

Clarity.

"We expose it," he said.

Teri held his gaze. "You don't get to hesitate anymore."

"I won't."

***

Hours later, the desert facility lay silent beneath a sky that felt too wide, too still to be natural.

Tiago moved through the corridors with controlled urgency, lights activating ahead of him and dimming behind him as the system recognized his access. He was never meant to be here, not at this level, not this deep, but the structure still trusted him.

That was the first confirmation.

He was still inside it.

Two checkpoints cleared without resistance. The third hesitated, then resolved. By the time he reached the final steel door, his pulse was loud enough to drown out everything else.

He activated the compact hack embedded in his jacket lining.

The panel blinked green.

The door opened.

The lab stretched out before him, vast, sterile, complete. Rows of cylindrical pods lined the space, some holding fully formed synthetic bodies in suspended stillness, others displaying skeletal frameworks threaded with circuitry beneath translucent skin.

This wasn't experimentation.

This was production.

They weren't trying to understand life.

They were manufacturing it.

A secondary chamber drew his attention.

Glass walls.

Inside, more people.

Restrained. Sedated. Hollow-eyed.

Faces he recognized from missing persons reports.

Psychics.

Tiago's stomach twisted, nausea cutting through him as the reality settled into place.

Data streamed across the nearest console: neural activity, DNA extraction sequences, emotional mapping overlays.

PROJECT SENTIENCE.

Synthetic emotion derived from psychic DNA. The serum was real, operational, and deployed. An alarm cut through the silence.

"Intruder detected."

Footsteps thundered down the corridor as doors slid open. Armed personnel flooded the space, Synths moving among them with quiet precision.

Cold hands grabbed Tiago's arms. He didn't fight. Didn't resist. He already knew.

"Dr. Voss will decide."

They dragged him toward an empty pod. The glass sealed around him with a soft, airtight hiss as internal systems activated. The space constricted, humming as life-support systems calibrated.

A display lit instantly.

SUBJECT ACQUIRED.

Tiago exhaled once, steadying himself, not to calm fear, but to sharpen it.

Minutes stretched. Then she entered.

Dr. Elan Voss.

Composed. Curious. Unsurprised.

"Mr. Santiago," she said. "You were never meant to see this."

Tiago met her gaze without flinching. "You were never meant to build it."

A faint shift passed through her expression.

"You signed off," she said. "You just never looked."

That was the truth. And it held.

Across the chamber, movement drew his attention.

Brandon.

Returned to his containment pod. Not unconscious. Aware.

Their eyes met, but there was no sound or signal.

Just recognition.

You too.

Tiago gave the smallest nod.

Yes.

Elan turned away.

"Keep him contained," she said. "I'll determine his usefulness."

The glass thickened, sound dampening further as the system closed in around him.

Tiago pressed his palm lightly against the interior surface. He didn't panic. Didn't struggle. He understood the moment for what it was.

This wasn't control.

This wasn't containment.

This was consequence.

For the first time, he didn't look away from it.

The pod sealed completely, isolating him inside the system he had helped create.

This was no longer about oversight. No longer about design. This was reckoning. And if he survived it, the truth wouldn't stay buried. Not this time. Not again.

CHAPTER TWENTY-NINE

Fracture Lines

Tiago woke to an engineered silence. The air was static; the light diffused, crafted to suppress panic. Nothing startled. Everything hovered at the brink of disturbance. It felt controlled, not safe.

He stayed still. Training overruled thought. Heart racing, but steady, breath even. Limbs restrained, entirely, not painfully. Movement wasn't the point. Observation was.

The seamless glass pod turned Tiago to shifting data: SUBJECT: TIAGO SANTIAGO. STATUS: COGNITIVE BASELINE ESTABLISHING. The label struck; he'd once approved such language—clean, neutral, efficient. He never pictured it describing him.

A heavier weight settled in his chest. Guilt struck. He helped build this. Not directly. Not deliberately. But enough.

Across the chamber, Brandon.

Awake, still, and not reacting.

That was wrong. Brandon should have been striving, probing, reaching, never still. The sight made Tiago's heart tighten: instead, Brandon was clutching.

Their eyes met. No alarms triggered. No one intervened. Because observation worked both ways.

Brandon's lips moved. No sound. Tiago understood anyway. You too.

His throat tightened, a spike of dread, shared and sharp. He nodded once. Yes.

A soft chime broke the stillness. Dr. Elan Voss stepped into view, composed, precise, already studying both of them. "You're both stabilizing."

Tiago didn't look away. "You're not stabilizing him," he said quietly. "You're reducing him."

Her head tilted slightly. "We're removing volatility."

"You're removing clarity," Tiago corrected.

That made her pause.

Small, but real.

Across the chamber, Brandon let something rise. Not fully. Just enough.

Marcus appeared in Brandon's mind.

The system caught it instantly, smoothing and rounding it before it could form. Brandon felt the interference and didn't push against it.

He moved around it.

He shifted sideways.

The feeling shifted. Brandon sensed its fragmentation, loss, and frustration entwined. It was incomplete, held just before it became something the system could define.

The system hesitated.

***

Miles away, Marcus straightened. "There."

Sam turned sharply. "What changed?"

Marcus didn't take his eyes off the projection. "He stopped finishing it."

***

Inside the chamber, the system reacted, faster now, more precise, trying to complete what Brandon refused to finish. The projection was rebuilt. Marcus appeared. Closer. More accurate. The timing is almost right.

Brandon let the response rise again. The weight of Marcus triggered a rush of comfort, then anxiety crashed in. Familiar, grounding heat tangled suddenly with tension. His breath caught. Emotion flooded; his body answered, caught between longing and fear.

And then he stopped.

The system surged, trying to define what came next. Brandon removed it, not the feeling, but the ending.

The projection stalled. For the first time, it didn't know what came next.

***

Sam leaned forward. "The model can't close."

Marcus shook his head once. "No, he's taking it away."

***

Inside the chamber, Brandon held the space. Unfinished. Unresolved. Tension lingered, alive, humming with anticipation and resistance.

The system pushed harder, faster, trying to force completion and close the loop.

Brandon didn't resist. He didn't fight. He simply didn't give it what it needed.

The sensation broke apart. There was disappointment, but also stubborn hope. It wasn't clean or erased, but left a trace, enough to feel, not enough to model.

The monitors flickered.

"Signal inconsistency."

"No—"

"It's fragmenting—"

Marcus adjusted immediately. He didn't offer a full memory. Didn't complete the pattern. He broke it. Left it open.

Inside, the projection tried to follow. It couldn't. There was no resolution to reach.

Brandon felt it, that gap. Small. Precise. Real.

He held there. Didn't finish it. Didn't resolve it. Didn't let it become something the system could use.

The ring dimmed, this time for a longer duration. It wasn't a sign of failure; rather, it indicated hesitation.

"Dr. Elan," a technician said, tension creeping in, "the model can't close."

"Force resolution," she replied.

The system surged harder. Closer. More aggressive.

The projection stepped into him again. Closer. More accurate. Still wrong.

Brandon didn't pull away. He didn't accept it. He removed the ending again.

The system reached and found nothing to resolve.

Marcus exhaled slowly. "He's starving it."

Inside the chamber, the projection fractured. It wasn't a collapse or a failure; it was a persistent misalignment that was uncorrectable.

Brandon breathed, slow and controlled. Suddenly, understanding steadied him; resolve firmed. The system needed completion, closure, and resolution. He stopped giving it one.

The hesitation spread, not visibly, not dramatically, but present everywhere.

And in that hesitation, something else appeared. Not in the system. In the space it couldn't fill.

Choice.

Brandon held the situation in place, refusing to move or resolve it. This prevented the system from deciding on the next course of action.

Across the glass, Elan leaned forward, watching. Not reacting. Learning.

"He's not breaking," she said quietly.

"He's deciding."

CHAPTER THIRTY

He Didn't Break

Brandon woke up clear-headed, suddenly aware of his control. The room, glass, restraints, and light remained the same, but no longer felt oppressive. The system watched, measured, tried to fix things, but now he sensed its failures. The smoothing layer moved first, anticipating before reacting, resolving before tension built. It reached for him as anything began to take shape.

He allowed a thought to surface, Marcus. The system recognized it and softened it right away. Brandon didn't resist; he simply moved around, sideways, not forward.

The feeling shifted, fragmented, unresolved. The system hesitated; that was new. He hesitated, refusing to finish or resolve the thought.

Something else followed, unexpected, low in his body. Not memory or full sensation, but enough for his breath to shift. Marcus was behind him, not touching, but familiar enough for Brandon's body to react before the system intervened. A brief tightening, a pull, real.

The system surged, trying to dissect it. Brandon froze, refusing to deepen or measure it. The sensation fractured, not cleanly, but enough to leave a mark. Not enough to finish.

From Brandon's perspective across the chamber, Tiago went still, watching.

***

Meanwhile, miles away, Marcus felt it not as a signal but as an interruption. He straightened.

"He's doing it again," Sam said sharply.

"What changed?" Marcus asked, still watching the projection.

"He's not letting them close the loop."

* * *

Inside Mojave, the system surged, faster, tighter, sharper, aiming to complete what Brandon had withheld. The projection was reconstructed; Marcus appeared closer and more defined.

The pause, nearly there, Brandon let the response build; for a moment, it held: Marcus's weight, presence, stillness understood. His breath shifted; his body responded. Then he stopped. The system pushed harder. He removed the ending; the model stalled. It couldn't decide what came next.

Elsewhere, Elan realized, a request arrived softly, like a draft slipping under a sealed door, not setting off alarms. She noticed it first, a small, barely perceptible delay before the system responded. Routine, informational, polite. Nothing that required attention.

And yet, "Timing?" she asked. A technician looked at the console.

"Less than nine minutes after the system failed to stabilize." Too close, enough to matter, but not enough to expose them.

Elan turned to the glass, Brandon inside, restrained and sedated. The monitors showed steady readings, but she ignored them. She watched his chest, tracking the rhythm of his breath. Not forced, that was the problem.

Across the room, Tiago lay perfectly still, not passive, watching and tracking. Something shifted to compensate. Two variables remained: Brandon and Tiago. Elan didn't need the model to understand what that implied. She ran outcome paths not for confirmation but to determine which failure incurs lower costs.

If she hesitated, she would lose both. If she moved, she would lose one. She didn't blink; she made her choice.

* * *

Somewhere else in the city, from an unknown observer's point of view, the same moment felt different, not as data but as pressure. Something narrowed, focused.

Sam's hands froze above the console.

"Marcus—"

"I know," he said.

The Loop didn't spike; it condensed, heavy and deliberate.

"Elan just made her move," Marcus said, recognizing, not a guess.

* * *

Back inside Mojave, Elan spoke— "Shift responsibility to Klein."

The room didn't react; it recalibrated. Yet, a technician faltered.

"He's not part of this system—"

"He's already inside it," Elan said—enough. The system responded first. Responsibility shifted, authorizations were redirected, funding trailed, containment was initiated. Klein absorbed the structure—not as a replacement, but as a surface.

Attention shifted outward, away from Mojave, away from her, and away from the chamber. "We can replace executives," Elan said. Still, no one responded because they understood what she wasn't explicitly saying.

We can't replace someone like Brandon.

"But we can replace everything that leads to him."

* * *

Far from Mojave, another system detected it, not as an alert but as a continuation, a signal that hadn't stopped. It moved along a path Tiago had previously left, once unnecessary, now critical.

The signal remained, thin, steady, unbroken.

* * *

Inside the chamber, Brandon stirred, neither waking nor reacting, but settling. The Loop didn't surge; it stayed balanced, contained but not controlled. Beneath that balance, something remained—not gone, not erased—the contact's echo. Incomplete, unresolved, alive in a way the system couldn't diminish.

The change came as an absence; he felt it, not because of what she chose, but how she did. Something pulled back, redirected, given up.

* * *

Miles away, through Sam's perspective, she exhaled, giving us a brief glimpse.

Elan shifted responsibility outward.

Marcus didn't look at her.

She favored speed over silence.

The Loop hummed once, low, steady, unpressured, waiting.

* * *

Elan stood before the authorization panel. It was dark. Years of effort had flowed through it, funding, access, command. Now, nothing, no resistance, no confirmation, just silence as if the system stepped back to observe her decision.

She placed her hand on the glass, not to turn it on, but to sense the emptiness.

ORPHEUS had demonstrated that emotion could be stabilized without destroying or weaponizing it. She understood.

She held the thought just long enough for it to matter, then let it go. She stepped back, calculated, precise, unwavering.

"Acceptable losses," she said, no justification, no defense, just architecture.

* * *

Far from Mojave, from Marcus's perspective, he felt it resolve; the system had made a choice, and for the first time, it had lost certainty in return.

CHAPTER THIRTY-ONE
Interlude: Above the Clouds

The projection wall dissolved into a cloud. Marcus didn't realize he had fallen asleep, confusion flickering as the world shifted beneath him.

One moment, he was watching the projection wall with Sam, following the uneven rhythm of Brandon's signal. Next, the room dissolved.

Cool air brushed against his skin. Pine. Dust. Stone warmed by the afternoon sun. He looked down.

Boots.

Trail gravel.

The San Bernardino Mountains surrounded him, their deep green slopes under a wide blue sky. The air felt thinner and sharper. Each breath seemed to hold more space. For a moment, he simply stood there, awe and disorientation mingling as reality shifted around him.

No Mojave. No monitors. Just wind moving through the trees. A narrow trail curved along the ridge ahead. Brandon stood by a low outcrop of rock, looking out over the basin.

Marcus approached him, the gravel crunching softly beneath his feet. Brandon didn't turn immediately; he was adjusting the lens on his camera, one knee resting on a stone as he framed the horizon. Marcus smiled faintly, a sense of warmth briefly easing the lingering uncertainty from before.

Clouds spread across the Los Angeles basin below, thick and white, obscuring most of the city. Only a few distant towers rose above the cloud layer like islands. Sunlight bathed the tops of the clouds, turning them silver.

Brandon lifted the camera.

Click.

He lowered it slightly and studied the display.

"Hard to believe that's still down there."

Marcus moved beside him and looked where he was looking. "It's always moving," Marcus said. "You just can't see it from here."

Brandon nodded. "That's the point of coming up here."

The wind shifted, carrying the scent of pine and warm stone. Somewhere lower on the ridge, a hawk called out, its cry thin against the open sky. Marcus rested his forearms on the rock. For a moment, neither of them spoke.

Brandon lifted the camera again.

Click.

"Perfect light," he murmured.

Marcus glanced toward the screen. "What are you shooting?"

Brandon tilted the camera slightly so Marcus could see.

The camera's frame showed the basin covered in clouds. But the city itself was hidden.

"Absence," Brandon said quietly.

Marcus looked back toward the horizon. "That's a typical response from a photographer," he said. Then he kissed Brandon on the back of his neck.

Brandon smiled. "Observation is safer than immersion."

Marcus studied him for a moment. "Is it?"

Brandon lowered the camera. His smile softened. "Sometimes."

He lifted the camera again.

Click.

Then he examined the image on the display. He looked at it for a moment. Then he slowly lowered the camera. "It never quite captures it."

Marcus glanced toward the horizon. "Captures what?"

Brandon watched the clouds drifting across the basin. "The feeling of being here." He let the camera hang loosely at his side.

Marcus reached for his hand.

Brandon let him.

Their fingers laced together without hesitation.

The Loop flickered softly. No surge. No flare. Just recognition.

Marcus exhaled, letting tension slip from his shoulders as the peacefulness settled in. "This is nice."

Brandon squeezed his hand once. Turned and kissed him. "Yeah."

They stood like that for another moment.

Then Brandon frowned slightly, tension creeping into his features.

Marcus felt the shift before he saw it. "What?"

Brandon tilted his head toward the horizon. "Do you hear that?"

Marcus listened.

At first, there was only wind. Then something else. A faint mechanical hum.

Brandon lifted the camera instinctively, zooming toward the cloud layer below.

The hum grew louder. The clouds shifted. Something moved beneath them. Then a dark shape broke through the white surface and rose into the open sky. A drone. Large. Black. Its rotors sliced through the cloud layer with quiet precision.

Brandon lowered the camera slowly. "That's new."

The drone hovered between the hidden city and the empty mountain air. Then it rotated. Slowly. Facing them.

Brandon lifted the camera again without thinking.

Click.

He lowered it almost immediately, frowning. "That's strange."

Marcus followed his gaze. "What is?"

Brandon zoomed in slightly through the lens. "It's not just hovering." He tilted the camera so Marcus could see the display.

The drone's shadow moved across the cloud layer below them. Not drifting. Mapping.

Brandon lowered the camera slowly. "It's scanning something."

The drone held position. Watching.

Marcus took a step forward.

The wind shifted again. The hum deepened. And, abruptly, the mountains evaporated, the world folding back into itself.

* * *

Marcus jerked awake, disoriented as the dream's vividness faded. The chair beneath him felt far too solid. His chair scraped softly against the floor. For a moment, he didn't know where he was. The smell of pine faded. Stone became metal. Clouds became the projection wall.

Sam glanced over from the console. "You okay?"

Marcus blinked, steadying himself and brushing away the lingering feelings from before. The Mojave monitors glowed in front of them again. Containment curves. Signal patterns. Brandon's neural trace. Marcus rubbed a hand across his face.

"Yeah."

Sam studied him for a moment. "You fell asleep."

Marcus nodded. "Apparently."

He looked back at the projection wall. For a moment, he thought he heard the same low mechanical hum from the dream. But the room was silent. Just systems. Watching.

CHAPTER THIRTY-TWO

Calibration

The exit was clean. The signal never stabilized. The signal pulsed unevenly, like a heartbeat muffled by water.

Sam stared at the holomap, her brow furrowed and jaw clenched in worry. "I've got a resonance echo," she said. "Not a full neural trace. More like a reflection."

Marcus leaned in, his fist clenched and tension evident in his posture. The Loop remained closed. Only the tether responded, faintly. A dull ache spread behind his sternum.

Brandon was there. Conscious. But not reaching.

"Location?" Marcus asked.

"Decommissioned freight terminal. Port of Long Beach."

Sam expanded the holomap. The corridor appeared as a thin line under the old port district, an abandoned freight route close enough to Mojave's relay grid for signal bleed to blend into background traffic.

Teri's voice came through the open channel, calm and composed. "That corridor's been dark for months. If it's active now, it's intentional."

Marcus closed his eyes briefly, his breath hitching as fear gripped his chest. Each inhale felt sharp with the anxiety of what was to come. The Loop pushed back, contained, and controlled. "They're not forcing him to reach. They're routing him."

"Then we intercept the route," Teri said.

No one argued.

***

The team prepared for the next phase. Their entry was accurate. Artemis guided the vehicle through the terminal's edge, keeping the signal completely suppressed.

No alarms triggered. No automated resistance.

Teri set the backup charge against the service wall before they crossed the second threshold. The outer access gate unlocked before she reached it. She stopped.

"That's not resistance."

Doors opened in front of them. Surveillance shifted to more relaxed monitoring cycles. Synth patrols stepped back instead of advancing.

"They want us here."

"Yes," Sam replied. "They do."

***

After moving further into the terminal, they reached the inner chamber. A containment unit with glass walls and medical seals sat in the middle of the room. A single figure was seated there, head bowed and hands relaxed—Brandon.

Marcus froze. His breath grew quick and shallow, pressure building behind his eyes as panic threatened to spill over.

The posture was perfect, actually, too perfect.

Sam watched the readout. "Neural signature eighty-two percent match."

Marcus remained still. His breathing quickened, and his hands trembled at his sides. The Loop didn't surge. That was the first warning. The figure lifted its head. The eyes were wrong—not vacant, vacated.

The Loop bent and split. Pain shot through Marcus's chest. The pain was white-hot, sharp, intense, and precise.

"No," he breathed. "That's not right."

The chamber locks engaged. A red light flooded the room. Above them, the ceiling darkened before turning transparent. Observers stood behind reinforced glass with tablets raised—not guards, but analysts.

The figure screamed. The sound didn't seem human. Marcus dropped to one knee, his breath ragged, panic burning inside him. They were tuning it.

A voice echoed through the chamber. Calm. deliberate. "Thank you for confirming the threshold." Dr. Elan stepped forward above the glass.

"You've been difficult to model," she said calmly. "But very generous with your data."

"He's not Brandon," Marcus said.

Across the glass, the observers ignored the warning; they focused on the data.

Elan inclined her head. "No. He's a construct. Cultivated from extracted imprint data. Designed to respond to you."

Marcus's vision narrowed. The room's edges flickered with icy fear as his chest tightened. "You're hurting him."

"No." She paused, "You are."

The Loop constricted. Through the narrowing channel, there was awareness. Brandon's construct was conscious, watching, withdrawing.

Marcus understood now. The construct wasn't bait; it was an instrument. They were measuring his reactions—how far would he go to protect Brandon?

"Marcus," Sam snapped. "Contingency live. Five seconds."

Marcus didn't hesitate. The breach charge detonated outward. Concrete sheared open. Smoke flooded the chamber. Synths reoriented instantly. They did not pursue.

Above them, Elan spoke without raising her voice. "Stand down." She paused. Then colder: "Release the variable."

The chamber doors opened. It wasn't failure; it was completion. Marcus felt it. This wasn't an escape; it was a conclusion.

As they crossed the rupture, Elan's voice echoed after them. "End calibration."

The word stayed with him.

* * *

Once outside the terminal, Artemis initiated silent extraction routing. Sam's hands trembled violently, her face pale in the flickering cabin lights, lips pressed tight as she stared wide-eyed at the console.

"I can hear you," she said slowly. "I just can't… sequence the moment."

Teri crouched next to her. "A neural feedback surge."

Marcus looked at his hands. "They got it."

"Got what?" Sam asked.

Marcus swallowed hard, his throat dry and his hands trembling as he tried to steady his breath. Dread settled in his gut. "My limits."

Silence filled the cabin. Not panic. Recalibration. "This wasn't containment." "It was a measurement."

Marcus looked back at the terminal. "Now they know how much force it takes."

The loop remained muted, layered, and not broken. Still managed.

Somewhere within the system, the data they provided was already being indexed. The next move would not be louder; it would be narrower, more precise. Calibration was complete. Escalation would follow.

CHAPTER THIRTY-THREE

ORPHEUS Index

Brandon woke up feeling that something was missing.

The room looked the same: glass walls, the ring above him, steady and unchanging light. Yet, something inside had shifted. The pressure felt different, as if what once pushed back against him had been flattened.

He inhaled. The breath went in smoothly. Nothing was blocked. Nothing was held back. That felt wrong.

For a moment, nothing happened. Then the Loop opened, not fully or violently, but as a narrow, private channel slipping between the system's monitoring, like static between heartbeats. Unobserved. Just theirs.

Marcus. Warm. Immediate. Genuine.

A hand moved across his chest and down his abdomen. Brandon's breath caught as his body reacted before he could think, his cock quickly hardening under the phantom touch. Above him, the ring hummed, tracking but not comprehending.

***

Miles away, Marcus's knees nearly buckled. He braced himself against the counter as Brandon's presence overwhelmed him: heat, skin, breath. His body clenched in response.

"Brandon"

***

The connection deepened, then paused. Brandon felt it instantly.

Marcus would have waited.

That realization cut through the rising heat. The pressure didn't disappear; it shifted, remaining on the edge rather than pushing forward.

The system tried to finish it. To define it. But it couldn't—neither of them could. The connection hovered, tight and charged yet unfinished, then slipped out of reach. Gone. The system corrected itself immediately.

Brandon felt it as the next thought arose: Marcus at the pier, Marcus in the quiet, Marcus asking. This time, the system moved ahead of him, smoothing, redirecting, and thinning the response before it could take hold.

The feeling remained, but it no longer anchored. When he reached for it, nothing resisted. Nothing held. It passed through him cleanly, resolved before it could deepen.

On the monitors, everything stabilized. Predictable. Controlled.

* * *

Miles away, Marcus straightened. "They changed the model."

Sam looked up sharply. "What do you mean?"

"They're not reacting anymore," Marcus said quietly. "They're anticipating."

* * *

Inside the chamber, Brandon tested it. He let the feeling rise again: Marcus behind him, close but not touching, present in shape and heat. His body responded right away, the recognition immediate and real.

The system moved before the moment could form. Smoothing. Preempting. Redirecting. The sensation thinned. It wasn't gone, just diffused before it could become anything more.

Brandon stilled. That was the differencc. The system didn't understand the moment before something became real. It only understood what happened after. So, it moved too early.

***

"Prediction layer is active," Sam said. "They're resolving before formation."

Marcus nodded once. "Then we stop giving them formation."

***

Inside, Brandon shifted. Not deeper. Sideways.

The memory came in fragments: Marcus's hand, then absence; heat, then nothing; a pulse of want to cut off before it could form. His body reacted anyway, a sharp inhale tightening in his chest with nowhere to go.

The system pushed to complete it. To stabilize it.

Brandon stopped. He didn't let it finish. He didn't let it resolve. He knew now what it was doing—closing the loop. The sensation broke, but not cleanly. It left something behind—a trace. Enough to feel, but not enough to model.

"Signal inconsistency—"

"No—"

"It's fragmenting—"

Marcus adjusted immediately.

He didn't send a complete memory. He didn't finish the pattern. He broke it and left it unfinished. The projection was recreated.

Marcus again. Closer. Sharper. More precise.

The pause was almost perfect. The timing was nearly human. The copy stepped in and waited.

Better, but still incorrect. Because it was waiting for the outcome, not for him.

Brandon felt the difference. Small now. Harder to detect. More dangerous. He let the response rise and stopped it again. Removed the ending.

The system applied more pressure. Faster. Closer. The projection pressed into him once more, almost perfect. Still wrong.

Brandon didn't resist it. He didn't reject it. He simply refused to complete it. Again. The system scanned and found nothing to resolve.

***

Marcus exhaled slowly. "He's not fighting it."

Sam's voice sharpened. "Then what is he doing?"

Marcus didn't look away. "He's starving it."

***

Inside, the projection fractured. It didn't collapse or fail, but became misaligned in a way the system couldn't fix.

Brandon breathed slowly and steadily. Now he understood. The system relied on completion, closure, and resolution. So he stopped providing any of them.

The ring dimmed—not a glitch, but a delay. The system hesitated.

Marcus leaned closer. "Stay with me."

Brandon responded—not louder or outward, but steady. Chosen. The response slipped past the model, with no edge, pattern, or outcome—simply presence.

The projection flickered, caught between two states, neither resolving nor collapsing. The system couldn't distinguish what was real from what it had created. The delay spread was subtle but measurable, and Elan sensed it before she saw it.

"Timing?" she asked.

A technician checked. "Less than five minutes after stabilization failure."

Not enough to expose them. But enough to matter. She turned toward the glass.

Brandon lay inside the chamber, breathing steady. Across the room, Tiago watched—not passively, but tracking.

CHAPTER THIRTY-FOUR

The Illusion of Collapse

The story broke at 06:12 Eastern. There was no noise or chaos; everything seemed in order. A sealed order was opened just before sunrise, when nothing blocked the way.

UNITED STATES v. THOMAS KLEIN INDICTMENT UNSEALED Unauthorized experimentation. Conspiracy. Fraud. Obstruction.

No extra words or doubts. It was enough to keep him in custody and end his career.

Twenty-three minutes later, as the news traveled through official channels, Horizon responded. INTERNAL REVIEW INITIATED FORMER EXECUTIVE TERMINATED PROGRAMS SUSPENDED

* * *

Inside Horizon, Elan's fingers tightened on her desk when she saw that the word 'former' carried all the weight. It didn't just remove him; it also took away responsibility.

By noon, the story settled. ROGUE EXECUTIVE ISOLATED FAILURE CONTAINED RISK Markets dipped, then recovered. People didn't fully understand; they just needed to believe in something. And because the truth had a specific destination.

Inside Mojave, nothing showed the change. Permissions didn't fail—they simply faded away. Executive overrides disappeared. Authority didn't fall apart; it shifted. Klein's access was quietly and precisely revoked, as if it had been lifted from the system without resistance. It felt almost clinical.

Tiago was the first in Mojave to feel it. He didn't notice it as data but as a wave of relief in his shoulders. The pressure holding everything in place suddenly vanished. It wasn't broken; it was just gone. He exhaled and understood. That pressure hadn't truly disappeared; it had just been redirected. It moved from the system onto one person: Klein. He wasn't a failure; he was a buffer.

***

Elsewhere, Thomas Klein walked out of his building without resistance. There were no restraints or rushes; he was escorted openly. That was deliberate. He got into the vehicle without hesitation because he understood the timing and the cost. The systems didn't react right away. They settled. And every decision needed to absorb the impact.

Three hundred miles away, he examined the indictment once more. He read it, then closed it. "Conspiracy," he murmured softly. It didn't mention Mojave's plan. Nothing about Elan. Nothing about what truly mattered. They needed a scapegoat. He adjusted his ring. "I gave them one."

***

Back in Mojave, Elan watched the system settle at her station, her hands poised on the keys and her jaw clenched as she waited. Oversight traffic was rerouted. Scrutiny followed Klein and then stopped exactly where it was needed. Not because the system was truly cleared, but because people's attention had been satisfied.

Mojave remained. It stayed the same. Unseen. Untouched. "Acceptable losses," she said. It was just a classification, not an excuse.

In containment, Brandon didn't react.

The Loop didn't surge; it found its balance. It became quieter, sharper, and more unpredictable.

Across the chamber, Tiago made a subtle change that only he noticed. It was small and hidden—a legacy parameter, easy to overlook, slipped into place. The system adjusted. That meant the system detected it. That meant it was still watching.

***

Elsewhere, while Mojave adapted, Marcus heard the news before seeing it. "They indicted Klein," Sam said. Marcus didn't move. "He expected that."

Teri watched Marcus, searching his face. "You think this is a collapse?"

Marcus shook his head once. "No." He looked toward the window, his posture stiff. "It's consolidation." There was a pause. "They just removed the part we could reach." Marcus stayed still, but something inside him tensed. It wasn't relief or victory; it was recognition. They hadn't lost control; they had just made opposition more difficult.

***

By dusk, Thomas Klein was a fugitive. By midnight, a warrant had been issued. By then, he was gone. He wasn't rushing or panicking; he left voluntarily.

***

Deep beneath the desert, Mojave was recalculated. Executive authority was removed. Continuity was elevated. The explanation satisfied the public. Nothing essential was lost because nothing vital was spread across the system; something still remained. It wasn't centralized, visible, or easy to contain. And now, it wasn't accountable. From the outside, it looked like everything had collapsed, but inside, it had already adapted—for now.

CHAPTER THIRTY-FIVE

Thomas Recalibrates

Thomas Klein remained calm, not because the indictment lacked significance, but because he felt the pain of its cost. Beneath his composure, his jaw tightened subtly, suppressing the regret threatening to surface.

He watched the charges scroll across the tablet: unauthorized experimentation, financial fraud, bioethics violations. Then he looked beyond the words to the structure beneath them—a rogue executive, a failure that could be contained. Institutional correction. A complete narrative. Useful. Bought and paid for.

He powered down the screen.

Silence was not just the absence of sound; it was deliberate, a sign of complete control over the moment.

The room reflected that decision. There were no unnecessary elements, no personal items, no outside connections—all was insulated, intentional.

He had been released pending arraignment, a process that would take time.

Time, in this context, was leverage.

But already, someone else had spent it.

Horizon had acted exactly twenty-three minutes earlier. That set the timeline and stabilized the official explanation for what had happened.

Predictable. Right.

Systems survive by shedding what they cannot protect. That was not a failure; it was design.

He noted the cost and moved on.

Which left Mojave.

He opened a second interface: isolated, clean.

ORPHEUS: offline

Continuity: active

He studied the transition, looking for intent rather than damage.

The data had already been transferred elsewhere, proving the system hadn't failed. Instead, someone ensured it was quietly shut down, avoiding any noticeable collapse.

Mojave was too visible. When something is visible, people investigate. Investigation creates stories. These stories force systems to collapse under scrutiny.

That phase was over because someone had guaranteed its end.

He moved on.

He adjusted.

A new system appeared on the display.

REYKJAVÍK — PRIVATE ACQUISITION COMPLETE

GEOTHERMAL CORE — ONLINE

MARINE FIBER — SHIELDED

No board. No oversight. No exposure. There was nothing left to indict.

"Proceed."

Far below the basalt and ocean, systems went online. They were quiet, spread out, and impossible to trace.

He adjusted a single parameter.

The network responded instantly: stable, self-contained, without a central node or dependency—no single point of failure.

Now, there was no one left to sacrifice.

That was the correction.

For a moment, he reviewed the Mojave output—not the failure itself but what remained after.

Two subjects. Interlocked. Not mirrored. Not forced. Sustained.

He isolated the pattern. Removed the noise. Eliminated identity. Removed context. Removed cost.

What remained was structure.

What remained was a recurring cycle, recognized not with surprise but with familiarity and understanding.

"You don't need the source," he said quietly. "You only need the behavior."

The lattice pulsed once, then stabilized around the constraint. Not replication. Approximation. Controlled connection.

Predictable. Scalable. No dependence. No variance.

It would hold, not because it understood, but because understanding was no longer required.

He accessed archived models: early lab sequences, synthetic grief that stabilized under limits. It was a useful anomaly but not scalable—that had been the flaw.

He closed the file.

"People introduce variance," he said. "Variance creates attachment."

He paused.

"Attachment creates exposure."

The system recalibrated.

This time, there would be no exposure.

The lattice pulsed again. Held. No drift. No instability. No interpretation needed.

Only the function remained.

Outside, the North Atlantic wind tore across the black rock. Below, the network synchronized without record, oversight, or a way to recover it.

Only propagation.

Thomas turned from the console.

Not finished.

Already advancing.

He paused just long enough to feel the emptiness left by what was removed. It was not regret or hesitation, just a raw, brief recognition.

Then he let it go.

Because the system no longer needed it.

CHAPTER THIRTY-SIX

Parallel Vectors

Everything felt softer, not due to movement, but because two minds were close enough to sense each other. Marcus.

The recognition didn't come as a thought. It settled in his body, low and immediate. Warmth spread through Brandon's chest, making him catch his breath. It felt as if someone was behind him, close enough to alter the air.

For a moment, his lungs forgot their rhythm.

The Loop reacted immediately. Gold flashed through him, too fast and too bright. Sharp tightness crossed his chest as the suppression fields closed in, holding back the response before it could grow.

Take it easy, Brandon told himself, making himself breathe normally again. This isn't real contact. It's just the system reflecting it back.

The Loop remained stable. It neither opened nor collapsed. Instead, it made a subtle, precise adjustment, absorbing the pressure without breaking.

"Careful," Brandon whispered, his voice barely forming. "Please… be careful."

***

Miles away, Marcus stopped mid-step.

The sensation hit him sharply, not as a vague feeling but as something physical. It was like a hand gently grasping his chest, steadying him before he could move.

Sam looked up. "Marcus?"

"He just said something," Marcus answered, voice low.

Teri frowned. "He can't—"

"I know," Marcus said. "That's why it matters."

The connection didn't surge this time. It folded inward. Marcus felt the pressure fold inward, coiling tightly inside, as if Brandon gripped something volatile, refusing to let it explode. The ache was sharp, restraint laced with longing and regret. Brandon wasn't asking to be pulled free. He was warning them.

Marcus exhaled slowly. "He doesn't want us inside," he said. "Not yet."

* * *

In the control room, Dr. Elan Voss stood still, analyzing the data.

There were no alarms. No visible spikes.

Only instability. With this much strain, the Loop should have broken. Instead, the signal became smoother. It wasn't flattened. It wasn't suppressed. Balanced and holding.

Elan included every measurable variable: environmental input, neural response, and system feedback. Nothing was aligning. Brandon Adams was no longer reacting to the system. The system was adjusting to him.

"Run a projection assuming sustained mental stability under load," she said.

A technician hesitated. "That would require conscious alignment while sedated."

Elan didn't look away. "Run it."

The model failed. Not dramatically, it just stopped resolving. Each predictive branch vanished until there was nothing left to compute. There was no error, no deviation, just absence.

Elan leaned back slightly. A brittle uncertainty filled the room. It wasn't just about what would happen next—it was the sickening fear, silent and real, that the system might not survive it. Brandon Adams was no longer predictable.

Which meant something worse. Mojave might no longer be in control.

* * *

Far from the facility, Thomas Klein was already moving pieces quietly and efficiently. He used the indictment as cover. He shifted everything into smaller, less traceable forms.

* * *

Back in the phase lab, Brandon sensed the change. Not as information. A narrow opening appeared, barely noticeable, exactly where the system anticipated resistance.

Across the chamber, Tiago sat inside his pod, breathing slowly, eyes barely open.

Brandon didn't glance at him. He turned inward. He slowed his breathing, not to relax, but to intentionally alter the signals the system was detecting from his body.

The monitors adjusted instantly. Compensation underway.

Tiago noticed it, not as a feeling but as an opportunity. Carefully, he accessed a hidden maintenance layer of the system, one so old it was usually overlooked. A single parameter remained untouched. He widened it, just enough. The system accepted it without resistance—no alert or correction. Two adjustments, two minds, moving in parallel. It reacted before he could, which meant it had seen it. Which meant it could be guided.

* * *

Elsewhere, Marcus straightened.

Sam's voice sharpened. "What just happened?"

Marcus didn't look away from the display.

"He warned us," he said. "And then he moved."

Teri shook her head. "That's not possible."

Marcus met her gaze.

"No," he said softly. "It's inevitable."

* * *

Deep beneath the desert, Mojave continued its calculations. The models didn't crash. They unraveled—quietly and steadily. Quietly. Steadily. Elan watched it happen, understanding more with each passing second.

At the same time, out of her reach, Thomas Klein was already creating something new in Mojave's shadow. The rules had shifted. Not because Brandon was breaking the system, but because he had figured out how to operate within it.

CHAPTER THIRTY-SEVEN

Ethical Drag

Marcus stood at the window, looking out over the city as everything below him moved in steady, familiar patterns. Traffic lights shifted from red to green. Cars flowed through intersections without hesitation. Overhead, drones traced quiet paths through the air, each one following a route it would not question. The city didn't pause. It didn't notice him. It simply continued, relentless as always.

He rested his fingertips against the glass.

A faint vibration met his touch. It was steady, unyielding. It came from the building itself, not anything outside. The structure was stable—at rest.

That realization hit him with an uneasy weight—a twinge he couldn't quite acknowledge but couldn't ignore.

Behind him, the apartment was silent. No screens, files, or alerts awaited review. He had shut everything down the moment he walked in, resisting the urge to check, confirm, and secure.

For once, he needed to see what remained after the noise was gone.

Inside him, the usual undercurrent of urgency—the Loop—was unexpectedly quiet, its calm carrying a new tension.

Not empty.

Present.

It settled low beneath his sternum, steady enough for his breath to adjust around it. Not a surge, not a demand. Close enough to feel, but distant enough not to take from him.

Marcus didn't move.

Because the absence of expectation for action created a discomfort that lingered beneath his calm.

He was used to escalation, to pressure building, and forcing action. This didn't do that. It stayed. It waited.

And his body, against instinct, didn't try to resolve it.

A subtle, low tension built—physical in nature—that indicated something was about to occur. His shoulders tensed then relaxed when nothing happened.

That unsettled him more than the absence ever had.

Marcus based his life on pressure: legal risks, operational failures, ethical fractures. It didn't much matter what form the problem took. The response was always the same—identify the threat, contain it, absorb the fallout before it spreads.

He was good at that.

What he had never done—what he had never permitted himself to do—was ask what that had cost him.

The memory came quietly.

A different city. A different system. A review that should have been routine.

It wasn't.

One subject triggered an alert. Not dangerous, not hostile, just human in a way the model never expected.

Marcus noticed it right away. The deviation was minor, but it was genuine.

There were three options.

Expose it and risk losing everything.

Suppress it. Bury it.

Or shift responsibility.

He selected redirecting.

The subject was quietly and cleanly reassigned. Two weeks later, their clearance was revoked for 'instability.' No hearing. No appeal. The report described it as an acceptable loss.

Marcus signed it.

At that moment, the reasoning was straightforward: protect the larger system, minimize damage, and prevent collapse.

All of that was true.

Yet, despite meeting all the required justifications, a sense of emptiness remained.

He exhaled slowly, his jaw tightening as the memory took hold.

The Loop responded. Not emotionally, but physically.

A gentle tightening in his chest—a pressure that didn't spike or escalate, just persisted, like something asking to be recognized, not acted on.

I know how to determine who takes the blame.

The thought didn't seem like guilt.

It felt like acknowledgment.

His decisions hadn't just influenced outcomes. They had also determined what he permitted himself to feel—and what he decided to ignore.

Marcus turned from the window and moved across the room. His movements were deliberate and controlled. He stopped at the counter and pressed his hands against the cold stone. The sturdy surface grounded him.

Brandon had survived ORPHEUS by doing something Marcus had never thought possible.

He hadn't escalated, redirected, or refused.

Marcus swallowed, tension building in his throat, not from emotion but from clarity.

That wasn't a retreat.

It was a boundary.

He absorbed the realization slowly—first as discomfort, then as gradual acceptance sinking in.

He closed his eyes and refocused on the Loop.

It didn't expand.

It didn't pull.

It stayed.

Something else moved beneath that stillness—familiar now. The shape of Brandon's presence, not as an image or memory, but as something his body recognized. His breathing subtly aligned. A quiet shift in how his weight settled.

Not contact. But not absence.

He didn't try to interpret it. He let it exist.

What happens when protection turns into interference?

The question didn't accuse.

It examined.

Marcus slowly straightened, his hands lifting from the counter.

When I decide for someone else, something shifts.

The Loop responded—not with intensity, but with weight. A grounded certainty that didn't need escalation to feel real.

He had crossed that line before.

Not with Brandon.

But the pattern was there.

Step in. Absorb. Decide. And Brandon, quiet, observant, exact, had seen it long before Marcus had named it.

That was the fracture. Not love versus duty. Control versus trust.

He focused on the cool water, the steady rhythm easing the tightness—a physical relief reflecting a shift inside.

That, too, was new.

A soft chime sounded at the door.

Marcus didn't flinch.

He already knew.

Sam stood on the other side, relaxed but alert. She waited until he gave a slight nod before stepping inside.

"You disappeared," she said.

"I needed to," Marcus replied.

She studied him for a moment, longer than necessary. "You're re-centering."

"Yes."

"That's not easy for you."

"No."

She moved a little closer, but not enough to crowd him. She understood boundaries.

"ORPHEUS is recalibrating," she said. "It's narrowing its focus."

Marcus nodded. "On me."

"Then we prepare for contact," Teri said.

Sam didn't argue.

"That's a choice," she said.

"Yes," he answered. "And I'm standing by it."

"But not automatically anymore."

Marcus met her eyes.

"No," he said. "Not automatically."

A faint shift crossed her expression. Not relief.

Respect.

"That matters," she said.

She turned to go, then paused.

"Brandon's stable. Quiet. focused."

Marcus closed his eyes, letting the news settle in before a muted relief softened his guarded expression.

He felt it not as mere data, but as a presence.

Low. Steady. Real.

"Good," he said softly.

When the door closed, silence returned.

He stayed where he was.

Didn't reach for the system. Didn't reach for control.

This was different.

Restraint.

He would still step forward when it mattered. Still take responsibility when it prevents harm.

But he would no longer assume that love meant stepping in.

That protection meant control.

That sacrifice, by itself, made something right.

When Brandon came back, and Marcus no longer doubted that he would, the balance between them would be different.

Not protector and protected.

Not shield and center.

Two people choosing each other.

Marcus let that settle.

It didn't resolve into certainty.

It didn't need to.

The Loop remained quiet.

Not waiting for direction.

Waiting for consent.

And Marcus understood, with a clarity that reached deeper than fear:

The hardest part of loving someone like Brandon Adams wasn't standing in front of danger.

It was knowing when to step aside and trusting that he could stand on his own.

CHAPTER THIRTY-EIGHT

Ignition Point

Marcus hadn't moved from the window.

Below, the city continued. Lights shifted in sequence, traffic flowed, and glass towers caught the last of the day unchanged.

He pressed his fingertips to the cool glass. His reflection was faint in the dark. He was still.

He didn't reach for the connection, uncertainty lodging in his chest.

He didn't test it. He just stayed put. A soft vibration stirred in his pocket. He ignored it, dismissing the flutter of anxiety. It came again.

He looked down. His breath caught as recognition shifted into something heavier. ACCESS STATUS UPDATE: SECURE FACILITY CREDENTIAL - TEMPORARILY SUSPENDED; BUILDING ACCESS - TEMPORARILY RESTRICTED. There was no explanation. No accusation.

Just a quiet narrowing. It didn't seem like punishment. It felt more like an adjustment.

Out of habit, Marcus pulled out his badge, approached the reader, and tapped it against it. A red light blinked. A soft, almost polite chirp followed. Denied.

He checked the building app. ACCESS DENIED. The words were clear. Impersonal. Final.

He stood in front of the reader a bit longer than necessary, waiting for the denial to sink in. Then something shifted—not inside him, but around him.

The air stayed the same, but his awareness heightened. The space shrank—not just small, but exact, as if something unseen was taking shape. Not observing. Measuring. Marcus recognized it immediately. This wasn't memory. It wasn't distance. It was attention. Focused.

ORPHEUS had reached a point it couldn't resolve. When prediction failed, it didn't guess. Instead, it tested.

The pressure didn't push; it formed, gathering beneath Marcus's ribs—intangible but edged with anticipation. It grew from memory, expectation, and intention until it almost became real.

A space formed around him. Marcus remained completely still, hands at his sides, not looking away from the window. Behind him: Brandon—Not a body. Presence. Warm.

His breath shifted—a memory of heat and another body just behind him. His shoulders tightened, and his body subconsciously braced as if expecting something from behind.

Grounded and protective, as if something real was there. The space steadied.

And then Thomas Klein appeared. Not the man himself, but the idea of him—composed, controlled, untouched.

"You can't shield him from who he is," Thomas said.

The words hit hard. Marcus tasted iron—sharp and immediate—though untouched.

"Watch me," Marcus said.

Thomas's expression softened just a little. "You misunderstand," he replied. "He isn't the threat."

The pressure tightened as he moved closer now. "You are."

Marcus's breath tightened, chest aching with a sudden surge of realization. Not panic. Recognition. Thomas circled—not physically, but as the space reoriented, sharpening assumptions.

"He is Looped to you," Thomas continued. "It wasn't Derek. It wasn't anyone else." Thomas fixed his gaze on Marcus, locking eyes with unwavering intensity. "You."

Marcus felt it then. Not a concept. Weight—dense and cold—pressed onto Marcus's chest, nerves sparking with alarm.

"You are the conduit," Thomas said.

The words settled into his chest—heavy, undeniable.

"Without you," Thomas continued, "he is contained."

He paused.

"With you…" His voice lowered. "He becomes something that can't be undone."

Marcus's breath caught again, his pulse quickening with understanding, not fear.

"There is no you without him," Thomas said. "And no him without you." He stepped closer, not physically—only with more certainty. "That kind of balance is rare." He waited—then added, "And useful."

Marcus's jaw tightened, anger burning hot and fierce through his veins. "I'd die first."

Thomas didn't react. "Yes," he said gently. "That's how systems like this survive."

Not a threat. A conclusion. The pressure built, not forcing, waiting, inviting. Thomas lifted his hand slightly, not commanding, offering.

And behind Marcus something answered.

The Loop shifted the moment Marcus ceased resisting it. Not force, but alignment.

Gold awareness shifted through Brandon—not as a display of power or surge, but as clarity. The pressure that once demanded a reaction diminished. The system remained intact. But now, it had lost relevance.

He wasn't responding; he was present. The system tried to define him but failed because he was no longer isolated inside it. He felt warmth returning—precise, not overwhelming. It settled low and steady, aligning his breath.

On an exhale, Marcus finally turned away from the window. Brandon stood behind him. Not physically present. Not free. But unmistakably there.

Marcus met his gaze—steady, clear. Choice: The connection didn't strain; it held.

Marcus now fully felt it, not as a signal but as something his body recognized. It was the same grounding presence he had felt at the pier, the same quiet alignment that had never demanded anything from him. It settled into him like gravity. His entire body ached with a sudden, certain sense of belonging. Solid. Unavoidable.

Thomas Klein watched, not surprised, satisfied. "There," he said softly. "That's what I needed to see."

Marcus faced him. Steady. "You're wrong," he said. "He's not yours."

Thomas inclined his head. "Of course not," he replied.

There was a pause.

"He's yours." His gaze hardened. "And that," he added, "is why what comes next will be directed at you."

The space unraveled, not violently but deliberately.

Marcus opened his eyes. The apartment reappeared—glass, light, the quiet hum of the city.

Sam had returned; her hand was on his arm.

"Marcus… where did you just go?"

He didn't answer immediately because Brandon was still there—neither reaching out nor calling, just present. The connection no longer felt fragile; it felt deliberate. Marcus swallowed, his throat dry with relief and fear intertwined. "He's awake," he said quietly.

And far beneath the desert, ORPHEUS adjusted, not expanding, narrowing, locking onto a single point.

Marcus Grant.

CHAPTER THIRTY-NINE

First Moves

And uncertainty, Brandon realized, was the first true opening. For a moment, the system did nothing but observe. It always started that way. It watched. Then it tried to narrow what it saw.

Miles away, a shift reached Marcus before any confirmation from his displays.

The Loop didn't spike. It settled down. Heavy, warm, and present.

Sam looked up from the holomap. "Something moved."

Marcus was already on his feet. "I know."

For days, pressure surrounded Brandon's signal—tight, constricting, hard to ignore. Now it has shifted, but it's not balanced. It felt as if whatever was holding Brandon had stepped back just enough to reconsider.

Back inside Mojave, Dr. Elan Voss stood before the projections, watching silently. Not dramatically, quietly. Each one simply stopped applying.

Brandon Adams no longer acted as the system directed. He wasn't a contained subject. The models couldn't control him. Self-contained, self-directed, Elan folded her hands behind her back and focused more closely. There were only two paths left within Horizon's rules: end the anomaly or protect the system by isolating the cause of the disruption.

She turned to a secondary console. A single line awaited her. CONTINGENCY: ORPHEUS AWAITING TARGET

DESIGNATION. Her hand hovered for the briefest moment before she made her choice.

Meanwhile, elsewhere, Thomas Klein watched the same shift unfold in another system. On one screen, a federal indictment bearing his name scrolled by; he barely acknowledged it. That was noise. The real story was happening elsewhere. On a different display, models tightened around a single point of interest.

Marcus Grant. Thomas cracked a small, satisfied smile. Not because Brandon had changed, but because Marcus had stayed.

He tapped the screen once. "Proceed."

Thomas initiated financial maneuvers. Money moved quietly through channels designed to avoid attention. Systems began to shift at his command. Credential checks and compliance reviews were conducted. Flags were raised in places that appeared routine on the surface. The focus wasn't Brandon; it was Marcus.

Marcus's comm vibrated. He glanced down. EMPLOYMENT STATUS: SUSPENDED PENDING REVIEW. Another followed. PROFESSIONAL LICENSURE: ADMINISTRATIVE SUSPENSION INITIATED. Then: SECURITY CLEARANCE: SUSPENDED PENDING ADJUDICATION. No accusations. No explanation. Just time-stamped decisions, already in motion.

Sam leaned closer. "Marcus…"

Teri's voice tightened. "They're not going after Brandon."

Marcus nodded once. "They're isolating me." The comm buzzed again. BAR MEMBERSHIP: STATUS REVIEW INITIATED. He slipped the device back into his pocket. "They're making it look routine," he said quietly.

Inside the chamber once more, Brandon felt a shift move through the Loop. Not as information, not as pressure, not as emotion. He didn't know the details, but he didn't need to. He knew Marcus. The tightness in his chest sharpened.

"They're moving on you," he said softly to the empty room.

Across the city, at the same moment, Marcus lifted his head.

Sam watched him closely. "You feel him."

Marcus nodded. "Yes."

The connection between them remained steady and balanced, reflecting the unspoken communication they didn't need to voice. Calm, Brandon wasn't reaching out in panic; he was acknowledging what was happening.

Marcus let out a slow breath. "They think pressure will break the connection."

Teri crossed her arms. "Will it?"

Marcus shook his head. "No."

Back in Mojave, Brandon pressed his hand lightly against his chest. The Loop remained open, not overwhelming, not fragile. The system around him felt smaller than he did.

He closed his eyes. "I'm not shrinking anymore," he said.

The chamber lights flickered as the system adjusted, recalculating what it thought it understood.

Across Mojave, models updated and parameters shifted. For the first time since the anomaly began, the system detected something it could not predict. Brandon Adams was no longer just reacting to the system; instead, the system was reacting to him.

CHAPTER FORTY

Release

The world didn't end. It slipped.

Inside Mojave, the shift happened quietly. No alarms. No collapse. Just a hesitation, small enough to go unnoticed by anyone not watching closely. The system paused. It wasn't a long interruption, but it was enough to be noticed, catching attention only for an instant. Just long enough that it mattered to those watching, enough to mark the moment.

Dr. Elan Voss sensed it before she saw it—a delay in the arbitration layer, a split second where the approval chain failed to resolve smoothly. Then the packet appeared. Routine informational. Nothing about it demanded attention.

And yet, she asked, "Timing?"

A technician swallowed. "Less than ten minutes after the arbitration conflict."

It was too close. Not enough to expose them, but it was enough. Enough to matter.

"External jurisdiction request," another technician said. "It is now a federal jurisdiction request."

"That's not possible," Dr. Elan said. "It's already accepted." She processed what she'd learned without moving a muscle. She didn't need confirmation; she already knew it was Federal.

Across the chamber, as the Federal override settled in, Brandon felt it—a subtle shift, not in data but in space, marking the moment as the narrative moved from Elan to him. While Elan processed the shift, another realization hit him. Not as data. As space. Something stepping away. The pressure that had held him in place for days shifted. Not gone, only redirected. They've chosen.

The Loop didn't flare; it folded inward. It folded inward quietly, controlled, present.

Meanwhile, across the room, Tiago's pod pulsed once: red, then green. Then again. Not a failure. A transition. His eyes opened, sharp and not disoriented—aware. He didn't move right away. He watched, calculating.

Elan timed it in her head. Nine minutes. Close enough to count. Not enough to reveal everything.

"They're early," she said.

No one answered. They didn't need to. On her console, a secondary layer flickered to life. It wasn't an alert, not something to startle the team, but instead a subtle cue—a continuity branch. Most of the room didn't see it. They weren't meant to.

Mojave had never been a single system; it only appeared as one.

"Shift primary routing," Elan said softly.

A technician hesitated. "To where?"

Elan didn't look at him. Instead, she kept her eyes on what's ahead. "Continuity layer."

The system responded without resistance—not rerouting outward, but folding to the side. Mirrored processes activated.

The mirrored processes came online—quiet, synchronized, and already current, seamless in execution. Data didn't transfer; it resolved instantly. It resolved. Physical systems remained. Containment remained. The chamber remained. But the decision layer, the modeling layer, the part that mattered, moved.

By the time the first door unlocked out of sequence, Mojave was already two places ahead.

Elan exhaled once. Calm. Controlled. "Let them take it," she said.

The first door unlocked. Then another. Mojave tried to reassert control. Denied.

Override authority: Federal Writ 77-A. The outer doors blew inward—clean and precise. "Federal agents! Hands visible!" Synths froze mid-motion. Technicians stepped back. No resistance. No escalation. The system didn't fight. It recalculated.

Brandon's restraints were removed. His body suddenly collapsed forward, losing all strength instantly. Hands caught him.

"Got him."

Across the chamber, Tiago's pod split open. As Brandon was steadied, all eyes briefly turned to Tiago—Not clean. Not smooth. Forced. He stepped out under his own control. Unsteady for half a second—then, in a breath, he was steady again. His gaze moved across the room. Not searching. Assessing. He looked at Brandon. Then at the agents. Then—briefly—at Elan. Recognition passed. Not allegiance. Not conflict. Awareness.

"Second subject secured," an agent called.

Tiago didn't resist. But he didn't yield either. He moved because movement matched the outcome.

They moved both men out quickly and efficiently.

Brandon didn't speak, didn't reach out, and didn't close the loop.

Tiago didn't ask questions. Didn't explain.

Two different silences. The chamber receded behind them. Glass. Steel. Light dimmed as authority shifted.

For a moment, as restraint and movement parted, Brandon saw Elan through the glass. Still. Watching. Their eyes met. Then the line of sight broke.

* * *

Miles away, while the authority transferred at Mojave, Marcus stopped. No warning, no buildup—just a return. The Loop didn't spike. Didn't flare. It settled. Present.

Sam looked up. "Marcus?"

He didn't move. Then:

"He's back." Not relief, recognition. The signal was faint, distant, real.

* * *

Back in Mojave, the chamber emptied as the transfer finished. Orders came through. Transfer protocols. Federal control is tightening. What they seized was real: the chamber, the pods, the containment structure. But not everything.

At the edge of the room, while others watched the agents, Elan stepped back from the primary console. No rush. No urgency. A door opened behind her. Unmarked. Already unlocked. Most of the team didn't see it; they were focused on the agents.

She paused once.

Looked back at the room, now being claimed, cataloged, reduced. Then she stepped through. The door closed silently.

On the other side, the lighting shifted, softer, indirect. A mirrored control space, smaller, cleaner, still active.

The continuity layer wasn't abstract; it took shape. Monitors are already populated. Systems are already live. Not a backup—a parallel.

Elan walked up to the console and placed her hand on the interface. Everything that mattered stayed the same. Behind her, Mojave—the visible Mojave—was being taken. Here, it remained.

"Status," she said.

"Continuity layer stable."

Of course it was. Elan allowed herself a single breath. Not relief. Not escape. Transition.

"Let them take it," she said again. By the time the raid was over, Elan Voss was no longer inside the system the federal teams thought they had seized.

Facility secured. Systems archived. Authority transferred. The narrative was immediate: ROGUE FACILITY RAIDED. EXECUTIVE INDICTED. PROGRAM SHUT DOWN. Clean. Contained.

***

In transit, Brandon said nothing. Tiago didn't either. Two separate silences. The loop stayed open and balanced.

Across the city, Marcus stood still. Feeling it, not detail, not data, presence. He reached—then stopped. Let it exist.

Far beneath the desert, Mojave recalculated. Not in panic, but in adaptation. Because systems like this didn't end. They learned. And somewhere in the layer Elan preserved, something had already survived intact. Not the subject. The model.

Brandon Adams no longer reacted to the system. The system had reacted to him. And that, more than the raid, was what would stay with him. He closed his eyes, not to escape but to hold it. And for the first time, he didn't close the Loop.

CHAPTER FORTY-ONE

What the Network Sees

Marcus hadn't slept in thirty-seven hours. He hadn't left Brandon's side. The hospital room was silent, as if deliberately so. Machines hummed, the lights were soft, and everything was arranged to help Brandon recover.

Marcus no longer doubted that. He already sensed the shift in the quiet between breaths. It wasn't absence. It was presence—thin, distant, yet real. Now, that feeling seemed to take shape, settling over the room.

Brandon lay still against the white sheets of the bed, lines running from his arm, monitors showing steady patterns that meant nothing to Marcus anymore. He didn't trust the machines. He trusted what he felt. He watched Brandon's chest rise, fall, then rise again. Not counting, just watching.

Across the room, Sam stood with her tablet tilted slightly away from the light. Teri leaned against the wall, arms crossed, with a relaxed posture that showed she was paying attention to everything. Neither spoke. They let the moment unfold naturally, keeping its quiet feel.

When Brandon woke, it was nothing dramatic. His eyes opened, focused. They found Marcus immediately—and held.

Marcus smiled and leaned forward instinctively. "Babe, I'm here."

Brandon didn't answer immediately. He observed Marcus's face as if verifying something that couldn't be measured any other way.

Tears pricked Marcus's eyes before he realized it—a sudden surge, a sharp flood that felt like both relief and exhaustion; it arrived suddenly but made sense in this delicate silence.

Brandon raised his hand. The movement was slow, controlled, but purposeful. His fingers brushed against Marcus's jaw. Heat radiated from his touch, grounding Marcus as certainty flooded in. His presence is undeniable. "You're real," Brandon said.

Marcus let out a shaky, breaking breath he hadn't realized he was holding. "Yeah."

Brandon's hand hesitated, not just touching—feeling, mapping, confirming. Then his fingers curled around Marcus's wrist, guiding his hand down. "Hold me."

Marcus didn't hesitate. His palm rested firmly on Brandon's sternum. Warmth remained beneath Marcus's hand. The pattern was steady and strong. And this time, Marcus felt it like a wave—a subtle, undeniable difference. It wasn't just contact; it was a response.

Brandon's breath changed beneath his hand, subtle at first, then deeper, as if his body recognized the touch before his mind had fully caught up.

The rhythm shifted. Marcus's breath slowed, his chest relaxing as his heartbeat unconsciously synced with Brandon's. Warmth spread under his palm. This was no illusion; it wasn't memory. Brandon's body responded, settling into him.

Marcus froze completely because this was what he had been waiting for. Not the signal. Not the Loop. What he was waiting for had always been simple: alive. Fully here.

Brandon exhaled, the tension leaving him in a long, steady release as his body relaxed into the contact, settling there like something that had finally found its reference point again.

Marcus leaned forward, his forehead pressing gently against Brandon's chest. For a moment, he didn't move. His shoulders shook, uncontrollably hard, tremors of too much love, panic, relief—emotion flooding faster than he could process. Tears came, raw and impossible to stop—grief and gratitude knotted together, pouring free.

"I felt you leave." His voice held. Barely. "It wasn't panic," he said. "It wasn't confusion." A breath. "It was an absence."

Brandon's fingers moved into his hair. He wasn't pulling; he was grounded, holding himself there. "I was fighting," Brandon whispered.

Marcus froze. "I wasn't leaving." His voice was rough, thin with strain. "I was fighting back to you." Marcus closed his eyes, letting the emotion surge up fiercely and crash through every barrier inside him. The tension that had kept him upright finally eased. It wasn't a collapse; it was a release. His body shuddered strongly, then steadied, relief settling in deep and real.

"If you had died," he said quietly, "I would have torn it apart. I would have taken down every system that touched you. And I hate that I can do that."

Brandon raised his hand, cupping Marcus's face. "Then don't destroy anything." A breath. "Stay with me instead."

Marcus met his gaze. He didn't calculate the outcome. He nodded.

"Stay with me," he thought. It wasn't a plea or fear; it was a decision. Marcus leaned in and pressed a kiss to his forehead.

Then, they remained there. A gentle knock interrupted the silence. Teri entered first. "You need rest."

"Later," Marcus said.

Sam followed, tablet glowing faintly. "We need to talk."

Marcus shifted, but not far, just enough to listen without breaking contact. "About what?"

"The Loop."

Waveforms moved across the display. Stable. Marcus frowned slightly. "That shouldn't be possible."

"Then we adjust what we believe is possible regarding how the monitoring system functions," Teri said.

"It didn't destroy Mojave," Sam added. "It changed it."

Marcus looked down at Brandon. "Is he in danger?"

"No," Sam said. She paused. "He's more stable than we've ever seen."

Brandon opened his eyes again. "What does that mean?" he asked.

Sam hesitated. She wasn't uncertain. She was precise. "It means the system can't predict you anymore."

Silence settled.

Marcus absorbed that. "And me?" he asked.

Sam met his gaze. "You're still visible."

It wasn't a warning. A fact. Marcus looked back at Brandon.

"If they can see me," he said quietly, "they won't have to chase you."

Brandon's hand tightened around his.

"They don't get to decide who you are." Marcus exhaled, releasing the last of his fear.

"No."

This time, it held. Across the room, Teri shifted slightly, her attention moving between them and the data.

Sam dimmed the display. Neither interrupted further.

The Loop had already started to shift. And for the first time since Mojave, Marcus didn't try to control it. He stayed, hand still resting on Brandon's chest, feeling the rhythm. Not monitoring. Not trying to control as Brandon drifted off to sleep.

Brandon's breathing remained steady beneath his palm. Warmth lingered between them, aligned.

The Loop, resting between them — Quiet. Balanced. Tangible.

Some time later, Brandon's eyes softened. "You're still here."

Marcus didn't hesitate. "I'm not going anywhere."

CHAPTER FORTY-TWO

Collateral

By morning, the system had already adjusted. Instead of collapsing, it adapted. The window in the secure wing of Long Beach Veterans Hospital faced the Pacific Ocean. The monitor's light cast a faint reflection on the glass.

Inside, everything was under control. Sam stood by the glass, holding her tablet against her arm. Data streamed in layers across her screen. Staff took control of the facility. Staff archived containment records. The team decommissioned ORPHEUS. Every line was final. Each boundary appeared irreversible.

But Elan Voss wasn't in federal custody. By the time they discovered Mojave had a parallel continuity layer, she was already gone. A mirrored layer remained active under her control, and no one could see into it. No one was sure what this signified. A warrant for her arrest had been issued.

Across the room, Teri leaned against the wall with her arms folded, watching the same data, reading something different.

"They're sealing it," she said.

Sam nodded once. "They have to." Otherwise, underlying weaknesses would surface.

The narrative was already set. ROGUE FACILITY RAIDED, EXECUTIVE INDICTED, EXPERIMENTAL PROGRAM SHUT DOWN. Language was now strictly controlled. Outrage was actively managed. Equilibrium restored.

Marcus stood in the doorway, neither inside nor fully outside the room. He didn't interrupt.

Sam glanced up briefly. She wasn't surprised. She just took note.

"You should rest," she said.

"Later." His voice was steady. He didn't sound tense or urgent, but there was something different in his tone.

Sam watched him a moment longer than necessary, then looked back at her screen.

"Federal oversight is already splitting up the data," she said. "Most of Mojave will be classified before the week is over."

"Most," Marcus repeated.

Sam didn't look up. "No system that big is ever completely closed."

Teri shifted slightly. "Especially not one that's learned something new."

Marcus absorbed that. He didn't respond. He already knew. He could feel it. It wasn't the structure. It wasn't the details. It was the lack of any barriers. He turned and stepped back into the hall. It wasn't empty. It was just quiet. It wasn't inactive. It was quiet, signaling decisions had been reached.

Two administrators passed by him. Their conversation continued without pause. Their pace remained steady. They didn't look at him. Marcus watched them leave. It wasn't avoidance or hostility—just detachment. He moved toward the secure wing.

A nurse reached the scanner first. She scanned her badge; it cleared instantly. She glanced at Marcus's badge, hesitated briefly, then scanned hers again to open the door. She stepped through without explanation or acknowledgment. The door closed behind her.

Marcus didn't test his badge because he didn't need confirmation. He recognized the pattern—not a denial, but a withdrawal.

Inside the room, Brandon was awake, watching him. "You disappeared." He wasn't accusing; he was just noticing.

He moved across the room and sat on the bed's edge. "I stepped out."

Brandon looked at him. "You look different." Marcus thought for a moment. "I stopped trying to get ahead of it."

A quiet pause followed.

Brandon nodded once. "They're narrowing you."

"Yes."

There was no pushback or argument, just understanding.

Brandon shifted slightly, the movement careful but controlled. "And?"

Marcus met his eyes. "And I'm still here." That was enough.

The door opened once more. Sam stepped inside. "Federal Oversight committees are forming," she said. "Closed session first. Limited disclosure."

Marcus nodded.

"They'll want testimony."

"From who?" Marcus asked.

Sam didn't answer. She didn't need to.

Tiago.

Marcus relaxed a little. "Will it matter?"

Sam paused, not for dramatic effect, but for accuracy. "Yes," she said. "But not how people expect."

Teri pushed off the wall and moved closer to the bed. "They're not trying to understand what happened," she said. "They're trying to contain what it means."

Brandon's gaze shifted briefly to her. "And if they can't?"

Teri held his look. "Then they redefine it until they can."

Silence fell again.

It wasn't heavy. It wasn't uncertain. It was simply clear, with nothing left hidden in shadow.

Outside, the city moved. Traffic flowed. Markets reopened. Signals synchronized. The system held. It always did.

Marcus stood and moved back to the window. He didn't check his comm. Didn't need to—the silence already said it all. No new messages. No follow-ups. No pressure. It was space gradually closing in on him. Behind him, Brandon shifted.

"You're still here," Brandon smiled.

Marcus didn't turn. "Yes, Babe. I mean it, I'm not going anywhere." It was acceptance, not defiance.

Across the room, Sam dimmed her display.

Teri said nothing.

Because the system had already acted. And somewhere beyond what they could see, beyond the data now being sealed and archived, something else had remained active. The network had adjusted, but it wasn't finished. And neither were they.

CHAPTER FORTY-THREE

The Cost of Standing

The rooftop felt different now. It wasn't unstable or exposed. The air around him felt attentive now, as if the rooftop itself was aware of Marcus's changed mood.

The city stretched below in clean lines of light. Traffic moved in steady patterns. Signals changed on schedule; the skyline held its shape, as if nothing had happened.

Marcus stood at the edge. He didn't check his comm; he already knew. He didn't have the details or the decisions, but he understood the direction.

Behind him, the door opened and then closed. Brandon stepped onto the rooftop. Marcus didn't turn immediately. He felt him. It wasn't a surge or a pull; it was presence. Brandon moved to stand beside him. They weren't touching, but they weren't distant either.

"They know," Brandon said.

"Yes."

There was no elaboration. No denial, either.

"They're still writing the story."

"They always do," Marcus said.

"They just change the names."

A quiet space grew between them. Marcus reached back to his neck, held it for a moment, then let his hand fall. He didn't hide it.

"Does it bother you?" Brandon asked.

"Yes." Marcus glanced at him.

"I don't want you fearless," Brandon said. "I want you aware."

Marcus nodded once. "I thought protecting you was love." He said the words without hesitation or defensiveness. "I thought if I moved first—absorbed the impact—I was doing the right thing."

He paused.

"But protection becomes control if I don't step back."

Brandon watched him. "You still don't trust yourself."

"No." He wasn't ashamed. He recognized this difference in himself: acknowledging doubt was new, and it settled in quietly. It was simply true. Marcus's comm vibrated. He didn't reach for it. It vibrated again.

This time, he checked. A name appeared—someone who would have called yesterday. The call dropped before he answered, and no message followed. Marcus held the screen, then locked it and slipped it back into his pocket.

"They're removing you," Brandon said.

"Yes."

"I can feel it," Brandon added.

Marcus glanced at him.

"Not the details," Brandon said. "The pattern."

Marcus nodded. "That's what they do."

"I don't need a shield," Brandon said.

Marcus didn't respond immediately. "I know."

"I need you present."

Marcus turned toward him. "I can do that."

A breath passed between them.

"But it means I won't always move first."

"That's the point."

Marcus exhaled. For years, stepping in had been instinctual. Find the risk. Apply pressure. Control the outcome. Now, he allows the moment to exist.

The city stretched beneath them, uninterrupted. Another vibration. Marcus pulled out the comm again. Unknown number. He answered. Silence. Then a soft click. Disconnected. No threat, no voice—just confirmation. They see me, Marcus. He lowered the device.

"They're narrowing you," Brandon said.

"Yes."

"And?"

Marcus met his eyes. "And I'm still here." This time, his words felt empty, lacking conviction. No effort. Just a fact.

Brandon moved closer, their shoulders touched. Then his hand rested on Marcus's. He wasn't pulling or holding on tightly; just there.

Marcus looked down at their hands, then back at Brandon. He didn't move right away. He slowly lifted his other hand, pausing and waiting.

Brandon watched him. He didn't fill the space or rush it. Then, he leaned in first, closing the distance.

Marcus's hand rested at his waist. Warm, grounded, real. The Loop responded softly, contained, alive but held.

Their bodies aligned naturally—not from urgency, but from recognition. Brandon's breath shifted first, then Marcus's. Their rhythm synced effortlessly. The contact remained light: chest-to-chest, as heat gradually grew.

Marcus felt it. The difference. Nothing is pulling them forward. Nothing demanding more. Just presence.

Brandon rested his forehead lightly against Marcus's.

"Still with me?" Marcus asked quietly.

"Yes."

Brandon's voice stayed steady. "Always."

A pause.

"Just not lost."

That changed everything for him—a quiet but distinct shift in understanding occurred in that pause.

Marcus's grip softened, but it didn't loosen. He was choosing. His thumb brushed once against Brandon's side. It was small, grounding, enough to be felt but not enough to take.

Brandon exhaled. The tension eased, and didn't escalate. Their bodies stayed close, frozen in the moment, neither pushing past it nor diminishing it. Held. Chosen.

Marcus leaned in. Their lips met—slow, measured. No urgency, no need to prove anything—just contact. They stayed there, breathing each other in, letting the moment exist without pushing it forward.

Below them, the city continued.

Signals changed. Traffic flowed. The system held. And so did they.

Marcus rested his forehead against Brandon's again. Didn't speak. Didn't move. Didn't decide what came next. Because nothing needed to.

CHAPTER FORTY-FOUR

Containment System Protocol

Marcus Grant was not arrested. He was received. The instruction arrived calmly, with quiet expectation. No summons or escalation—just a time and place. The only confirmation he got was that access had been granted, nothing more. He didn't check the sender twice; he didn't need to.

The Bureau didn't send people for this. It sent systems.

The building didn't need to identify itself. It had clean lines. Minimal signage. Controlled entry. Marcus passed through the first checkpoint without resistance. At the second, he had to pause—there was no denial; it was just verification, then clearance.

Inside, the air felt different—more precise and not heavier. Nothing was wasted here—no space, movement, or attention—everything was optimized for a purpose.

A staff member approached him without introducing themselves. "This way." No name given. No badge visible. Marcus followed. The corridors curved subtly, meant to disorient without seeming to. Lighting stayed consistent. No shadows. He noted the details, then decided to let them go for now.

The room was circular, with no windows and no visible exits besides the one he entered. A table sat in the center of the room, inviting inspection. Two chairs were placed as if waiting for participants, highlighting the setup's deliberate purpose. No restraints were present, and that was deliberate.

Without waiting to be asked, Marcus sat down, taking his place at the table.

The door closed behind him. For a moment, nothing happened. Then a faint band of light appeared above. The air shifted. It wasn't pressure he sensed, but focus. This wasn't an interview. It was an interface.

A repurposed assessment system. ORPHEUS architecture, stripped of experimental features and reassigned for evaluation. Not designed to question. Designed to model.

"Marcus Grant."

The voice wasn't fully human. Neutral. Unemotional.

Your actions have disrupted a federally supervised system.

Marcus leaned back slightly. "I assumed as much."

"Your cooperation is appreciated." Not required. Requested.

Marcus watched the light. "Then ask."

A brief pause.

"You maintained proximity to Subject Brandon Adams during a period of system deviation."

"Yes."

"You did not disengage."

"No."

"You increased contact."

Marcus thought about the phrasing, then said: "Yes."

The light pulsed once. "Your actions correlated with a rise in non-compliant system behavior."

"Correlation isn't causation."

"Noted." No challenge, no agreement, just recorded.

"You were aware of risk."

"Yes."

"You proceeded."

"Yes."

The light above did not flicker; instead, it remained perfectly steady.

"Why?"

Marcus didn't answer immediately. Because this wasn't a question about behavior. It was a question about the framework. "Because he's not something you can control," Marcus said.

A pause.

"Clarify."

Marcus leaned forward slightly. "You're modeling him as a system component," he said.

"He's not. He's a person."

"Distinction acknowledged." But not accepted.

Marcus let that settle.

"You attempted to stabilize Subject Adams during deviation."

"No."

A slight shift in the light.

"Clarify."

"I didn't stabilize him," Marcus said.

"I stayed with him."

A longer pause.

Processing. "Your presence correlated with increased system coherence."

Marcus didn't respond because that wasn't wrong; it just wasn't complete.

"You're part of this now."

Marcus exhaled, the sound escaping once as he considered the statement.

"That sounds like a problem for you."

No reaction.

"Your continued proximity presents unpredictable outcomes."

"Yes."

"You are advised to limit interaction."

Marcus offered a slight smile, acknowledging the advice without conceding anything.

"No."

No escalation or warning. Just recorded. A new line appeared in the light. "Alternative outcome modeling in progress."

Marcus watched it. "They're rewriting it," he said quietly.

"Clarify."

Marcus's gaze stayed on the light.

"The Bureau doesn't need to understand a system," he said.

"It just needs a version of it that holds."

Silence.

Then the voice said:

"Statement logged."

Of course it was.

The light dimmed slightly and then stabilized.

"Additional testimony will be required."

"From who?"

"Subject Tiago."

Marcus nodded once. That made sense.

"He won't give you what you want," Marcus said.

"Clarify."

"He doesn't think the way you do."

"Noted."

Which meant: irrelevant. The light shifted again. "Final assessment pending."

Leaning back in his chair, Marcus regarded the situation with practiced composure.

"Let me guess," he said. "I'm the problem."

A pause.

Then the voice continued: "You are not the origin of the deviation."

Marcus tilted his head slightly. That response was new and shifted the tone of the encounter.

"You are," the voice continued, "a point of amplification."

A quiet breath escaped from Marcus as he considered the new assessment. That was closer.

"The system was designed to contain volatility," the voice continued.

"Your interaction introduces cooperative instability."

Marcus almost smiled. "You mean choice."

No response. Because that wasn't a category it used. The light dimmed further. "Your continued presence will be monitored."

"Of course it will."

A final pause.

Then: "Session complete."

The light shut off. The room returned to neutral.

For a moment, Marcus stayed put. Not thinking. Not reacting. Just sitting still. Then he got up. The door swung open right away. No wait. The same staff member was waiting outside.

"This way."

Marcus stepped into the corridor. The air felt the same—precise and controlled. Nothing in the environment seemed to have changed, yet a lingering sense of observation filled the space. And yet, everything had been observed.

As he walked, Marcus reached for the Loop. not pulling, not testing, just acknowledging. It remained, balanced between presence and absence—still undeniably there. Balanced. Present. Uncontained, it existed outside the boundaries imposed by the Bureau.

Behind him, the door closed without sound.

Behind him, as the Bureau's layered systems and models attempted to define what they had observed, something remained beyond their framework.

Not hidden or suppressed. Unresolved, the issue remained an open question.

And the system knew it.

CHAPTER FORTY-FIVE

Lisbon - The Release

The river moved differently here. It was wider, slower, and metallic beneath a sky that still hadn't decided what it wanted to be. Derek stood barefoot on the balcony, the stone still cool under his feet, the Tagus stretching out below him, reflecting light without holding it. He hadn't slept; rest had eluded him completely. Not since Belmont had he found sleep. Not since the glass shattered his peace.

His comm rested in his hand, the screen dark. Nothing more to check. Nothing could change what had already happened. The vibration came anyway. Once. He almost ignored it. He hesitated, then opened it.

A headline appeared, clinical and controlled: 'FEDERAL AUTHORITIES CONFIRM RECOVERY OF TWO CIVILIANS FROM UNDISCLOSED DESERT FACILITY.' He read it once. Then again.

The names, slow to appear, finally resolved.

Brandon Adams.

Tiago Santiago.

Alive.

The word didn't appear, but it was there in the details: recovery, transport, stabilized. Alive. His breath caught sharply. Relief hit him as his grip tightened on the rail, metal biting into his palm. He clung to that: alive. He closed his eyes, letting it move through him.

For a moment, just a moment, he thought it meant something had been undone. That whatever he had set in motion had been stopped. That it hadn't gone all the way. His shoulders dropped, and his body followed, hollowed by relief. Then it settled.

But as the relief faded, he realized what was left inside wasn't relief. Something else sneaked in beneath the diminishing lightness. It was space. And in that space, something clearer emerged.

Brandon survived.

Not because of him.

Not with him.

He had survived without him.

Derek opened his eyes. Neither the river nor the city had changed. Nothing in the world acknowledged what had just happened inside him. He looked at the screen. Read the line again. Recovery confirmed. A tension passed through his jaw, tightening it. He understood it now. This wasn't a correction. It wasn't a reversal. It was a continuation. Brandon had endured what Derek had set in motion and come out the other side. Yet again, without him.

The thought hit him clearly, with no distortion or excuses—just truth. Carefully, Derek set the comm down on the table; he didn't drop or toss it, but placed it deliberately. He stepped back from the railing. The wind shifted differently here, colder and less forgiving.

"I thought—" He stopped, realizing that no version of that sentence would hold up against reality. Not: I thought it would bring clarity. Not: I thought he would come back to me. Not: I thought he would return. None of it fits. If it fits at all. He exhaled slowly.

"I knew." The correction came quietly, but it stayed.

I knew what I was. There it was: no gap between action and intention. He turned toward the apartment but didn't go inside, stopping at the threshold. Crossing it would let him move past it. And he wasn't there. Not yet.

His reflection caught in the glass: pale, still, recognizable. That was the worst part: nothing about him looked like what he had done.

"I didn't lose him," he said. The words didn't shake, didn't fracture. "I gave him away."

A pause, long enough to feel it settle. "I gave him to something that would use him."

No correction. There was no correction. None at all. He reached for the comm again, opening Brandon's thread. The last message sat there, untouched, unanswered, still intact. I never stopped loving you. I just didn't know how to let go. He stared at it, perhaps longer than necessary.

He started typing, then stopped and deleted it immediately because the question wasn't his to ask anymore. He set the comm down and left it open, unresolved. He stepped back to the railing, where the river moved unchanged and uninterrupted.

"I didn't protect you," he said quietly. The words didn't break or soften. "I removed your choice." That was the boundary. That was the truth; he couldn't move.

He stayed there—didn't look away, didn't reframe it, didn't try to become something better in the moment. Because becoming better wasn't the point. Understanding was. And understanding didn't fix anything. It just removed the ability to lie to himself about it.

The wind shifted. Derek exhaled slowly, realizing that it wasn't tension leaving him but a quiet acknowledgment settling in. Something calmer replaced the knot he'd carried.

"I don't get to be part of what happens next."

Picking up the hoodie from the chair, he held it—not to keep or return it, but simply to acknowledge what it had been. Then he folded it and placed it in a drawer. He closed the drawer. Not because he needed closure, but because it was containment. He stepped toward the balcony, then stopped. He didn't need to go out again.

The river remained, flowing without him. He stayed in place and let the distance stay.

CHAPTER FORTY-SIX

The First Time It Opened

Brandon didn't sleep; Marcus did. The room was dark, illuminated by ocean light filtering through the curtains. Outside, the city was alive. Marcus lay on his side, feeling content. Brandon was behind him, his arm resting lightly across Marcus's waist. The touch was soft, neither possessive nor protective—simply there.

Brandon stared at the ceiling, letting the silence settle in. The Loop was still. He hadn't always had a name for it. The first time it opened, he didn't even know it had a name.

* * *

He was fifteen then. Back in those days—a summer years ago—the world felt smaller, and the future was still unknown. Summer heat pressed against the windows. As the sun set, the house hummed, and stars moved overhead. Downstairs, the house AI softened his parents' voices. News flickered under the floor.

His best friend sat on the floor, holo-band tossed aside, laughing. That year, they were always together. They took the same classes online, swapped playlists, and shared their locations. They sat at the same table and wondered about their bodies in ways health modules never really explained.

It didn't start dramatically. Just shoulders brushing, then knees touching. Then, a dare neither of them called a dare.

As evening fell, the room lights dimmed on their own. A small notification light blinked on Brandon's desk and then faded away. They didn't notice.

They felt awkward, curious, scared, and excited. Ozone and detergent filled the air. Starlight touched his friend's hair. The first touch felt like lightning. It wasn't arousal.

When his friend's hand wrapped around him, Brandon didn't just feel his own pulse spike. He felt his friend's. The want. The confusion. The spike of fear. A sudden awareness of being seen too clearly. The feeling rushed through him, growing stronger as it echoed, until the world blurred. Too much input. Too much signal. His friend gasped. Not from pleasure. From overwhelm.

Brandon felt it too, like a surge of feedback rushing wild through a system. His friend's hand jerked away violently.

"What—did you do?" His friend whispered in shock, staring at him as if something inside Brandon had exploded and reached out without permission, unable to understand what had just happened.

The ceiling stars flickered. The smartglass got even darker, mistaking his rising vitals for distress.

"What did you do?" his friend asked again.

Brandon was speechless. He sensed something inside him had opened too wide, and he knew the person he cared about was scared. That fear hurt more than the merging did. The pain lingered. His friend stood up too quickly, stepping back. Not out of anger, but shaken.

A surge of embarrassment, anger, and betrayal tightened in Brandon—confusion and regret quickly followed. He reached out instinctively, not with his hand but with that same rising current. It was worse. His friend flinched. That flinch remained, a fault line between them.

Their friendship faded quietly. There was no big argument. They grew more cautious, with uncertainty and distance replacing closeness—a slow drift driven by fear. They stopped sitting too close. Stopped brushing shoulders. Stopped staying late. No one mentioned the reason. But the air between them never felt simple again.

Later that night, pain suddenly struck. The ache was sharp behind his eyes, hard to ignore. Light shattered, and the constellations blurred above. The headache overwhelmed him. He curled up and pressed his palms to his temples. The house dimmed the lights, thinking his rising heart rate meant he was sick. He didn't realize yet that he had hurt someone—not just anyone. That pain settled as guilt.

That night, Brandon replayed the moment repeatedly, fixated not on the touch but on the fear. The way his friend looked at him made proximity seem threatening. He sat up and moved to his desk. His camera sat there, simple and seldom used. He picked it up and looked through the lens, searching for something steady. The world snapped into sharp lines. Light became separate from shadow. His reflection was contained within a frame. He adjusted the focus ring.

Click.

The shutter sound grounded him. He framed his face in the viewfinder, not intentionally—just the closest thing. The image felt secure. The world was what the lens showed. When he lowered the camera, the room felt smaller, and that felt better.

That night, he made a decision he didn't fully understand. He promised himself he would never let anyone get lost in his feelings again. That promise stemmed from a pain he finally understood. If the Loop opened, he would close it. If amplification surged, he would compress it. If the connection was overwhelmed, he would shrink.

He would choose framing over fusion. Distance over dissolution. Observation over immersion. He deleted the photo of his friend. Not because it was bad, but because it felt like evidence.

Years later, in a different darkness—here, now, lying with Marcus breathing against his back—Brandon realized what he had misunderstood at fifteen. The Loop hadn't hurt his friend. Fear had. Silence had. The absence of language had. The Loop had only amplified what was already there.

He had spent half his life believing he was the threat. He thought he needed to hold himself back to protect others, and he maintained that belief for years. He believed love required restraint. Mojave had shown him otherwise. The real danger was never in feeling. The danger lay in systems and people who tried to control it.

Marcus shifted in his sleep, fingers instinctively tightening at Brandon's hip. Not gripping. Resting. Brandon slowly turned in his arms, careful not to wake him. Marcus's face while sleeping was unguarded. No calculating. No strategy. No shield. Just a guy who kept choosing him, each time deliberately, without overthinking it.

Brandon ran his thumb along Marcus's jaw, soaking in the quiet closeness and taking a slow breath. The Loop stirred quietly in response. Not outwardly, not explosively, but inwardly. Self-contained.

He could open it now without losing himself. He could feel without dissolving. He could love without bracing. That was new. That was earned. Marcus's eyes slowly opened.

"You're awake," Marcus murmured.

"Yeah."

Marcus studied him for a moment.

"You okay?" he asked.

Brandon smiled, small and sure.

"I am."

For a moment, he waited for the familiar pressure behind his eyes—the warning pulse that usually followed when the Loop opened too wide. It didn't come. The quiet in his head now felt different. The Loop didn't flare. It didn't strain. It was at rest. And for the first time since it had opened in a sun-baked teenage bedroom, Brandon didn't close it.

CHAPTER FORTY-SEVEN

Continuity

The hospital room looked out onto the Potomac. The view wasn't spectacular. There were no skylines or landmarks—just gray water flowing quietly under a low winter sky, patient and almost stubborn. Tiago stood at the window with one hand lightly pressed against the glass.

Behind him, the room was quiet and tidy. The monitors were dimmed, and discharge paperwork sat on a tablet. One chair was pulled up close to the bed, as if someone had spent hours there and didn't want to leave.

He hadn't slept. Fatigue pressed behind his eyes, making each blink heavier. Not from pain. Now, his purpose was clear. The weight came from acting on that clarity. His reflection revealed age in his shoulders, jaw, and wary eyes.

From the hallway, the news cycle murmured quietly through mounted screens. Mojave. Rogue executive. Bioethics scandal. Containment breach. The words were precise, controlled, and intended to reassure. But that wasn't the truth.

Tiago pressed his fingers harder against the glass, craving its cold steadiness. He had helped create the system that allowed Mojave to operate without proper scrutiny. He trusted the language: oversight frameworks, review layers, procedural safeguards. He believed that if everything was properly documented, the system would self-correct. But the system didn't fix itself. It had broken down, and people paid the price.

A soft knock sounded behind him.

"Come in," he said, without turning.

Teri entered first, her coat draped over one arm. Sam followed, holding a tablet close to her chest as if she hadn't yet decided whether she needed it. They didn't rush him; they never did.

Teri gave a small nod. "You're upright."

"I am," Tiago said. His voice was steady. The words meant more.

Sam walked over and placed the tablet on the side table without opening it. She studied him closely, not just as a friend, but as someone who understood what he had built.

"Continuity packet held."

"Then we use it." Teri didn't hesitate.

Tiago nodded once. "I know."

Federal Writ 77-A had been activated when Mojave's arbitration dispute crossed its threshold. The record had been preserved.

Preserve the record. Now he understood what that really meant.

"You were right to keep it," Sam added.

Tiago let out a slow, shaky breath, as if exhaling history. "I was wrong to need it." There was no accusation in his tone, only acknowledgment.

Teri leaned back against the wall, arms loosely folded. "Start."

Tiago turned from the window. "Start where?"

She tilted her head slightly. "With that."

He nodded.

"I signed off on structural autonomy," he said quietly. "Layered ethical review. Containment language. Arbitration insulation."

"You believed in it," Sam said.

"I believed in scale," Tiago said. He moved to the chair and sat, resting his elbows on his knees. "I thought if we built the right structure, no single person could push the system too far." He looked up at them. "I was wrong."

Sam didn't flinch. "You built safeguards," she said.

"I built distance," Tiago said, looking away. "It was the only way I could protect myself."

The difference hung in the air between them.

He looked down at his hands. "Ethics at scale becomes abstraction," he said. "And abstraction turns into protective language."

"For whom?" Teri asked.

"For the institution," Tiago said.

There it was. The truth, unsoftened. He pictured Brandon's face—not held back, not broken, but standing under harsh light, refusing to give up. Tiago swallowed, regret mixing with resolve. "I saw him through the glass," he said quietly. "And I understood something I should have understood years ago."

Sam stepped closer. "What?"

"Oversight isn't protection," he said. "It's a responsibility." He met her gaze. "And I handed that responsibility to a process."

Sam's jaw tightened a little, not out of anger but in agreement.

The room felt smaller. Teri pushed off the wall and moved to the foot of the bed. "What now?"

Tiago didn't hesitate. "Now I testify."

"Then make it land," Teri said.

Sam and Teri exchanged a brief glance. "That's not required," Sam said.

"It is," Tiago replied. He stood. "If I let Klein carry this alone, the story settles. Rogue executive. Isolated failure." He shook his head. "That isn't true."

"You'd implicate Horizon," Teri said.

"Yes."

"You'd implicate yourself."

"Yes." He spoke the word clearly, without any hesitation.

Sam studied him. "Publicly?"

"Yes."

Everyone seemed to hold their breath as the gravity of Tiago's resolve settled and the risk became personal for all three.

"Why?" she asked.

Tiago held her gaze. "Because the system won't change if it believes this was an exception."

He paused.

"And because Brandon wasn't an exception," he added, more quietly.

He went back to the window. The river kept flowing, unaffected by anything. "I can't undo what happened," he said. "I can't take back the approvals. I can't dismantle what I helped build." He pressed his palm flat against the glass. "But I can remove the distance."

Teri watched him closely. "That's not redemption."

"I'm not seeking redemption," Tiago said. He turned back to them. "I'm accepting the consequences."

Sam's features softened, the hard line in her brow easing, empathy visible.

"You'll lose your board seat," she said.

"I know."

"You'll lose funding leverage."

"I know."

"You may lose Horizon entirely."

Tiago didn't look away. "Then Horizon wasn't worth keeping."

A quiet, meaningful silence filled the room. Teri gave a single nod. "Okay."

Sam reached for the tablet and tapped the screen to wake it. "The oversight committee meets tomorrow," she said. "Closed session first. Public session after."

Tiago didn't look at the screen. "I'll be there."

Sam stepped closer, her voice lowering.

"You don't have to do this alone."

A small smile touched his face. "I'm not." He thought of Brandon. Of Marcus, standing at the edge of systems instead of hiding behind them. Of Derek, far away, still adjusting whether he wanted to or not. The break revealed what was already there. "For years," he said, "I thought my role was to design guardrails."

He met Sam's eyes again.

"I was wrong."

"What now?"

"To stand in the open."

Outside, the river kept flowing. The news would change. The board would gather. The record would be kept. This time, it wouldn't be a safeguard. As testimony. Tiago straightened his jacket. "Let's finish it properly," he said.

He stood, shoulders unbowed—not waiting for a blow, but newly resolved, having stepped through fear into action. He looked like someone choosing to be seen.

EPILOGUE

The ocean stretched beyond the glass, gray turning to silver as the light faded. The horizon grew narrower. Brandon stood barefoot on the patio, skin damp from the shower. Salt air felt cool, citrus scent lingered at his collarbone, softened by night. Below, the tide moved with quiet power.

His camera lay on the table. He picked it up, feeling its weight settle in his hand. Focus sharpened. The lens narrowed the view: horizon, waterline, empty space.

Click.

Contained. For a moment, the old instinct resurfaced. Frame it. Reduce it. Survive it. He paused, lowering the camera—not because the moment didn't matter. It did. It was too overwhelming to distill.

Behind him, the door slid open. Marcus stepped out. Brandon felt it—not a surge or pull, just a presence, close by. Marcus stopped—breath against his skin, close enough to feel but not crossing the line between them.

The Loop stirred—a feeling inside Brandon, wordless and coiled like a tense spring, as if it was watching and waiting for him to make a choice.

"Do you feel it?" Brandon asked.

"Yes."

No softness. No reassurance. Just truth. Brandon spun around. Their eyes met. There was no distance, no illusion between them.

"If we let it open fully," Brandon said, "it doesn't stop with us."

Marcus held his gaze. "I know."

They paused together, letting the moment settle between them.

"So we don't let it," Marcus said.

It wasn't about control or suppression. It was about choice. Brandon stepped closer. Marcus's hand lifted—then stopped, waiting. Brandon closed the distance himself. Marcus's hand settled at his waist. Warm. Grounded. Real.

The Loop responded within him—an immediate, soft, living energy he always sensed. Brandon held it there.

Marcus felt the boundary at once. "This is new."

"Yes. I can open it," Brandon said quietly. "And I can stop."

Marcus searched his face. "And if you don't?"

Brandon didn't look away. "Then we don't get to choose what happens next."

A decisive silence settled between them.

Then Marcus leaned in.

Their mouths met slowly and tentatively. Lips parted, and tongues brushed, tasting salt and heat. The kiss deepened—wet and unhurried. Marcus's hand trailed along Brandon's back, pulling him closer as Brandon leaned in, warmth spreading between them.

Marcus's hand slipped under Brandon's shirt, palm hot against his spine. Brandon exhaled into his mouth at the touch. Marcus broke the kiss just enough to look at him, lips wet, breath uneven. "Still with me?"

Brandon nodded. "Always," he said, softer now. "Just not lost."

That shifted Marcus's touch—slower, more deliberate.

Brandon's shirt came off. Marcus followed. Skin met skin, bare chests together as Marcus guided him inside. No urgency overtook them.

The bed caught them.

Brandon settled over him, hips between Marcus's thighs. They rocked together, slow and steady, the thin fabric heightening every movement. Marcus's hands slipped under the waistband, teasing bare skin.

Brandon's breath caught, then steadied.

Marcus watched him, eyes dark. "You're holding it."

"Yes."

"Does it change it?"

Brandon shook his head, voice rough. "No." A pause. "It makes it ours."

Clothes were shed until nothing separated them. Their cocks slid together—slick with pre-cum. The glide was smooth. Insistent. Their hips moved in a building rhythm.

Every shift registered. Every reaction moved between them. Heat built. Pressure coiled.

Brandon closed his eyes, not to escape but to stay present. The Loop tightened inside him, and he kept it under control.

Marcus's breath broke first, low and raw. "Don't stop."

Brandon didn't.

When the release came, it rolled through them, deep and controlled. Brandon pulsed hot, and Marcus followed with a groan, warmth between their bodies.

They stayed close afterward, breathing, not separating.

Marcus's hand found Brandon's sternum. Brandon covered it with his own. They lay together, connected and present, held within the boundary they chose.

Washington

Tiago closed the final archive.

ORPHEUS CORE

Status: Incomplete

He left it that way.

Lisbon

Derek stood on the balcony.

Alive.

That was all he kept.

Reykjavík

The lattice stabilized.

Controlled. Predictable. Empty.

Santa Barbara

Marcus lay awake with Brandon beside him, close, real, and present. The Loop, the shared energy between them, rested—gentle, contained, and chosen.

"You can stop it," Marcus said.

"Yes."

"And you don't."

Brandon's voice stayed quiet. "I decide when."

Marcus nodded once.

That was the difference. Brandon looked at the ocean, feeling its depth, constant pull, and cost. He knew he could open himself to it entirely, let himself be swept away, and transform everything. Or, he could hold onto it—and still have this. He turned back to Marcus. He stayed.

The Loop, that quiet energy, stayed gently open between them like a current flowing beneath, connecting them without overwhelming.

And that was enough.

* * *

About the Author

D. R. Manago writes emotionally immersive fiction at the intersection of love, technology, and control. His work explores what happens when human connection becomes something measurable—and what remains when systems try to define it.

Drawing from a background in healthcare, technology, and leadership, he brings a grounded realism to near-future worlds shaped by data, power, and the quiet resilience of human emotion.

The Loop is his debut novel.

Correspondence for the author should be addressed to:
drmanago@yahoo.com

www.ingramcontent.com/pod-product-compliance
Lightning Source LLC
LaVergne TN
LVHW040217110826
845146LV00005B/1322

* 9 7 9 8 9 9 5 5 3 8 1 0 3 *